THE MAN WHO COULDN'T BE

The Man Who Couldn't Be

Roderic Jeffries

Hodder & Stoughton
LONDON SYDNEY AUCKLAND TORONTO

British Library Cataloguing in Publication Data

Jeffries, Roderic
    The man who couldn't be.
    I. Title
    823′.914[J]   PZ7
    ISBN 0-340-39829-9

Copyright © Roderic Jeffries 1987

First published 1987

Published by Hodder and Stoughton Children's Books,
a division of Hodder and Stoughton Ltd,
Mill Road, Dunton Green, Sevenoaks, Kent TN13 2YJ

Photoset in Linotype Baskerville by E. P. L. Typesetting,
Beckenham, Kent

Printed in Great Britain by T. J. Press (Padstow) Ltd,
Padstow, Cornwall

Chapter 1

The fog – at that time of year called a freet by many of the local inhabitants – slipped across the land with deceptive speed. Nick didn't see it until he breasted the hill and began to freewheel down, yet by the time he reached the relatively level stretch of road at the bottom, the first wisps were already curling around the fresh spears of bracken by the side and many of the Herdwick sheep had vanished. The valley was fast becoming a place of infinite dimensions.

This, he thought, was all he needed!

That morning, Uncle Ben (not a true uncle, but a long-standing friend of his parents) had suggested it would be worth his while to cycle up to Steerson Tarn, one of the local beauty spots. He'd left the house at half-past two, after a very full lunch – Aunt Caroline was an excellent cook – and had reached the tarn in just under an hour. It had proved to be an irregularly shaped stretch of water, surrounded by trees, fed by a fast-running stream, and too cold to encourage a swim. Not being someone who could spend an endless time appreciating and enjoying any scene, however beautiful, he'd left after a quarter of an hour and had set off for home, carefully retracing his way through the initial maze of lanes. At least, that was what he thought he'd been doing until he passed a tumbledown cottage which he was certain he had not seen earlier . . .

The fog engulfed him, reducing visibility to metres and making it foolhardy to continue cycling. He braked to a stop, climbed off the bike, and began to wheel it along. As the road appeared in front of him and disappeared behind him, he had the fanciful thought that he was moving along in a small bubble of life whilst everywhere else there was nothing . . .

In the depths of winter, the steppes of Siberia must provide the same sensation. But there, beyond the bubble, there was something – wolves. Circling ever closer, waiting for their prey to weaken . . . He laughed aloud . . . It wasn't the depths of winter and the Lake District was not noted for its ferocious wolves.

The narrow lane turned very sharply right, so much so that it caught him out and he suddenly found himself in the middle of it. Hurriedly he crossed over to the verge. That was when he noticed the twin ruts in the soft grass. Curious to know what could have caused them, he came to a stop and stared into the fog. After a second or two it seemed to him that he could just make out a shape. He laid the bike down and went forward.

As the fog retreated, he found himself looking at a large, green car whose registration letters immediately, if only temporarily, caught his attention: NAW. The same as his initials. The driver's door was open and the inside light was on. Beyond the car was a dry-stone wall and it had crunched into this; the nearside wing was crumpled. Clearly the driver had been travelling too fast for the conditions, had suddenly come into the very sharp bend, had tried to get round and had failed, and the car had ploughed across the grass verge to hit the wall. Since there was no sign of the driver, it was reasonable to suppose he'd gone off for help. If he had as much luck as Nick had had in finding someone to give directions, he'd be gone a very long time . . .

There was a sound from within the car which made him start and it was a second before he identified it as a groan. He moved until he could look into the back where he saw a figure sprawled across the seat. The man's head hung half off the seat. He had a heavily-bearded face and he had received a nasty blow on his right cheek; there was a cut that was bleeding and a surrounding area of heavy bruising.

Nick had virtually no knowledge of first-aid, but of one thing he was certain, the man's head should be moved so that it no longer hung down. He pulled open the offside rear door and for the first time saw that the man's right leg was in plaster. They said that troubles never came singly, he thought, trying to concentrate on anything but the bleeding wound which made him feel slightly squeamish.

He went to move the man's head up on to the seat, but this proved far more difficult than he'd expected because of the angles involved. So did he try and move the whole body? But he was sure it was wrong to move an injured person unless this was absolutely necessary, for fear that there were internal injuries. So how important was it to raise the head? The man's breathing appeared laboured and this decided Nick; he put one foot just inside the car to gain a better purchase, took hold of the man's shoulders and slowly, carefully, exerting all his strength, managed to lift and to push until they'd gone back a little way; enough for him to raise the head up on to the seat.

The injured man did seem to be breathing slightly more easily now. For the first time, Nick studied his appearance. His hair, slightly curly, was as black as his full, neatly-trimmed beard and moustache; his cheekbones were notice-ably high; his nose was beaky; his complexion was dark; his clothes had an expensive look about them even when he lay in so ungainly a position. Foreign, Nick thought, making this snap judgement not on any one feature, but on them all com-bined.

The man moved with a quick, jerky roll that momentarily took him to his right and it seemed there was a chance his head would once more go over the edge of the seat; but then he rolled back to his previous position.

Nick said: 'Try to keep still.' He was very conscious of how little he could do to help.

The man groaned, mumbled something.

'I'm sorry, but I can't understand you. You've been in a car accident and have injured your face. The driver's gone off to find help and he'll be back any minute now.'

The man spoke and this time his words were clearer, but they proved to be in a foreign language which Nick couldn't identify.

7

'Can you repeat that in English?'

The man moved his right hand, as if trying to reach up to his injured cheek.

'Is there something I can do for you?'

There was a sound from behind Nick which made him think of a shoe striking a loose stone. He straightened up, imagining this was the driver returning. He began to turn, but then something hit him on the head and blasted him into unconsciousness.

Chapter 2

He seemed to be clawing his way out of some kind of a pit.
There was the sound of people talking and although the words
came through to him as a jumble, he became convinced they
concerned him. He wanted to ask them what they were saying, but when he tried to talk it seemed as if his tongue were
sheathed in cotton-wool.

A hand rested on his forehead and fingers gently slid open
his right eyelid.

'He's regaining consciousness.'

A pain which throbbed in time to his heart grew in a tight
ball at the back of his head. Instinctively, he went to reach up
and find the source of the pain.

'I wouldn't do that if I were you.'

His hand was returned and his fingers brushed a smooth
fabric that made him think of a sheet. That, together with the
fact that if he moved whatever he was lying on gave slightly,
convinced him he was on a bed. Why? And why was there this
throbbing pain in his head? And why was he weaker than a
half-drowned kitten? Some of the answers began to come. He
remembered the swirling fog, the very sharp bend in the road,
and the crashed car . . . 'What's up?' he mumbled.

'You were unlucky enough to be standing under a tree with
your bike when a branch broke off and crashed down on you.
A couple found you and came here, to Miss Thrayson's house,
and she phoned me. I'm Doctor Boshover. And now, no more
questions until we find out how things are with you.'

He was asked to move his fingers, toes, arms, and legs; he
opened each eye in turn and a light was shone into it; a hand
was held up in front of him and he was asked how many
fingers he could see . . . Did they think he was not yet out of

nursery school, he wondered resentfully. Was he suffering from any particular pain? He replied that his head felt as if someone was boring into it with a pneumatic drill.

'I'll give you something that should calm that down . . . Well, it looks as if you've been lucky and escaped with no serious damage. Are you up to sitting?'

He moved as he would normally have done and the pain flared so that he drew in his breath sharply.

'Are you sure he's not too bad?' asked a woman whom he presumed to be Miss Thrayson.

'Yes,' the doctor replied shortly.

He tried a second time to sit up and now moved slowly and carefully. Once in position, he opened his eyes. Standing by the side of the bed was a middle-aged man, a little overweight, dressed in a well-worn suit, with a round, pleasant face, and possessing the typical air of rushed, confident, medical authority. Beyond, at the foot of the bed, was a woman, older than the doctor, who looked flustered. The bedroom was large and furnished with some beautiful antiques. Through the sash-window, hung on either side with chintz curtains, he could see, since the fog had partially lifted, part of a well-maintained formal garden.

'Do you think he'll be able to tell us yet who he is?' asked the woman.

'Try asking him,' replied the doctor, in the slightly ironic manner which came from having had Miss Thrayson as a patient for many years and knowing her to be someone who wasn't nearly as helpless as she so often made herself out to be.

She moved closer to the head of the bed. 'Can you tell us what your name is?'

'Nick Woods,' he answered in a croaky voice.

'Do you live near here?'

'No. I'm just staying for a holiday.'

'I thought you must be. I've never seen you before. And even if my memory's not as good as it used to be, I never forget a face . . .'

10

The doctor interrupted her. 'Where are you staying, Nick?'

'With the Ransomes in Stillthwaite.'

'If they're on the phone, can you remember the number?'

'Stillthwaite four-one-six-two.'

The doctor turned to Miss Thrayson. 'Will you ring them up in a moment and explain what's happened? You can say it's all right for them to collect him right away.'

'Yes, of course.'

'I've some pain-killers in the car which I'll give you before I leave; he can take up to two every four hours if he needs them. When you see Mrs Ransome, say that everything seems to be OK, but it's important she keeps a close eye on him for at least the next twenty-four hours. If the headache increases in severity after taking the pills, or if there's vomiting, or his vision becomes at all confused, she must call in her own doctor immediately.'

The doctor spoke to Nick. 'You'll almost certainly be as right as rain this time tomorrow.' He smiled, a brief, professional smile. 'I'll be off now.'

Nick quickly said: 'Just before you go, do you know how the man in the car is?'

'What's that?'

'I was wondering how badly hurt the man in the car is?'

'Which man in what car?'

'The one which had skidded into the stone wall.'

'Would you like to tell me a bit more?'

Nick described what had happened. The doctor rubbed his chin with forefinger and thumb. 'You're quite certain about all this?'

'Well, of course. I mean, I can remember it clearly.'

'And rationally! . . . When you lost consciousness, you were standing alongside this car?'

'I thought I'd better lift up the man's head, but I didn't like to do anything more. He started to come round and mumbled, but I couldn't understand because he was speaking a foreign language. Then I heard something behind me and reckoned it was the driver returning. And that's the last I knew.'

11

'You're quite positive the noise came from behind you and not from above?'

'Yes, I am.'

'I see . . . I don't know, Nick, whether you really took in what I told you earlier. You were knocked out by a branch which broke off an old oak tree. So the sound you heard must have come from above.'

'Only it didn't.'

The doctor rubbed his chin again. 'Can you describe the sound again.'

'There were two, really. First it was like a stone being kicked by a shoe, then the stone hitting something.'

'It wasn't the noise a branch in leaf would make when it broke off and crashed down past other branches?'

'Nothing like that, no.'

'Don't forget that fog often distorts sounds.'

'Not that much.'

'Perhaps not.' However, the doctor obviously remained unconvinced.

Nick suddenly realised something important. 'It can't have been a branch falling; there weren't any trees near the car.'

'You weren't moved before I got to you and there was an oak tree close by and there was the branch which had been pulled off you. When I examined your head, I had to clean away bits of bark and leaves.'

'But there just wasn't a tree anywhere near,' he repeated stubbornly.

The doctor expressed his perplexity. 'It's all becoming somewhat complicated!'

'Don't you . . .' began Miss Thrayson.

He shook his head to show that he thought it was in the patient's interests not to pursue the matter any further for the moment. 'I must be off, Miss Thrayson, so if you'll come down with me, I'll give you those pills . . . and Nick, don't worry. Remember, a sharp knock on the head can do funny things to memories.'

They left the room. Nick slowly wriggled down to a lying

12

position and closed his eyes. Easy for the doctor to talk about not worrying, but was his mind really playing him that false . . .?

Chapter 3

Doctor Boshover's two hundred year old farmhouse stood on high ground and from it one had a view across a wide valley to the stark – and in bad weather, ominous – mountains on the far side. It was uncompromisingly rectangular in shape and was built of stone which had been rendered a sad browny-grey; from an aesthetic point of view it had little to recommend it, but in a winter gale, when the rain became so torrential it seemed as if the second Flood had started, its solid virtues became very apparent.

He swivelled the chair round and stared out through the window at the valley, a view of which he never grew tired – born only a few miles away, he believed this to be the most beautiful countryside in the world. His pipe was in his mouth, but the bowl was empty of tobacco; for years, his wife had been trying to persuade him to give up smoking and finally he had made the effort to do so. There were times when he found it a very difficult task . . .

He realised that he'd been tapping on the desk with the fingers of his left hand and, annoyed, he abruptly stopped. He'd always disliked fidgeting. But these days, when a problem went round and round in his head, he seemed more and more often to fidget . . .

'Blast it!' he said, as he reached over to the telephone.

There was a call from the kitchen: 'The meal's ready.'

'Just coming,' he shouted back. He picked up the receiver, realised he'd forgotten the number, took a small notebook out of the top right-hand drawer of the desk and consulted this. He dialled. When the connection was made, he asked if Detective Sergeant Johns was at home. Mrs Johns asked him to hold on. As he waited, he began to tap on the desk once more, but this time did not become aware of the fact.

'Evening, Doctor Boshover,' said Johns in his breezy manner. 'Something I can do for you?'

'Yes. Find the answer to a question.'

'What's the question?'

'Can a blow on the head so affect a person's memory that he not only forgets what did happen just prior to the blow, but clearly remembers a logical sequence of events which did not.'

There was a short pause, then Johns said: 'I'd have said that that was more like your department than mine.'

'On the face of things, you're right.' He'd put the pipe down on the desk; now, he picked it up by the bowl with his free hand and held the stem close to his mouth, as if about to start smoking. 'But I need to be sure of certain facts before I can come to any conclusion and I reckon these facts might well come into your department.' Briefly, he told Johns what had happened.

'On the face of things, then, the boy's memory must have flipped?'

'Would a blow which scrambled his memory to that extent have left him remembering a false but perfectly logical scene with such clarity?'

'Doesn't that bring us back to the beginning? Surely that's a medical question?'

'As with so many of those, the authorities hedge their bets when it comes to answers. But I'd raise a point. Suppose the boy's memory *is* correct, how would you square it with what's happened?'

'I could only suggest someone wanted to hide the fact that the car had crashed into the wall and so the scene was set to make it seem that the boy's story had to be a load of cods. And, by the nature of things, if everyone tells the boy so, sooner or later he's likely to start accepting that.'

'If someone had such a motive, you'd be interested in him?'

'Very interested.'

The Ransomes had been shocked by the telephone call from

Miss Thrayson, but they were level-headed people and when they'd arrived at her house they had acted so calmly that she had at first been rather upset by what seemed to be their callous indifference to events; only in the last few minutes, just before they left, had she seen Caroline look at Nick in a way that made her realise that their concern was hidden rather than lacking.

Back in Fawver Cottage, Ben helped Nick up to bed and then Caroline asked him if he felt like eating anything. When he replied that he was really quite hungry, she smiled delightedly and returned downstairs to cook him chicken breasts in a piquant sauce of her own devising.

Nick ate all the chicken and finished the meal with ice-cream topped with chocolate sauce and cream.

'One thing's for certain,' Caroline said, 'the accident hasn't affected your appetite.'

'No. Only my memory.'

'And the doctor said you were to forget all about that.'

'Have you ever tried to forget something?'

She smiled. 'I know. The harder you try, the more you remember it . . . All I can suggest is that you concentrate on a more interesting subject. What would it be in your case? Girls?'

'Cars,' he replied scornfully.

'But of course!' She laughed. She had a round face; large, very soft, brown eyes, a slightly snub nose, and a cheerful mouth. Nick always thought of her as a fun person, and that was a good description.

She sat down on one corner of the bed. 'There's something I want to talk over with you. Ben and I have been wondering whether to ring your parents and tell them what's happened, or whether it mightn't be better just to leave it for a bit. What are your feelings?'

'One thing's for sure, if you ring Mum right away, she'll worry whatever you tell her.'

'That's exactly what's been going through our minds. Even if we say you're almost back to normal already, Thelma will start thinking that really you must be seriously ill or surely we wouldn't have bothered to tell her. Then, the more we assure her, the more she'll become convinced that something is wrong. If you were seriously ill, of course we wouldn't hesitate, but as it is . . .' She waited, leaving him to make the decision.

His mother was one of those calm and level-headed people who normally accepted life as it came; but to this there was one definite exception and that was if either his father or he was ill. Then she became pessimistically convinced that tragedy was just around the corner . . . Tell her he'd received a smack on the head that had laid him out and left him with a scrambled memory and she'd insist on rushing up to see him, arming herself with a list of the most eminent brain surgeons in the country . . . 'I'm sure it'll be best not to say anything right away. Then maybe in a few days I could ring and just casually mention it, and since by then it'll be all over and done with, she won't be able to do much worrying.'

'I said to Ben that you'd a sound head on your shoulders.' She stood and picked up the tray. 'So that's what we'll do. And now I'll leave you. But don't forget, the first hint of any trouble and ring that bell.'

'I'm fine.'

'Good. And between now and sleep, keep your mind firmly on Ferraris.'

'Aston Martins.'

'I thought you said it was your ultimate ambition to own a Ferrari?'

'I've changed my mind since then.'

'And why not? What's the point of being wealthy if you can't change your mind? You will take me out for a drive, won't you, Nick? I've always wanted a fast car, but Ben says they're too dangerous. He's right, of course. But such fun to have the world rushing by . . . But for an old biddy like me, that's talking nonsense!' She left.

She was certainly no old biddy. He'd met a number of people who were younger in years, but considerably older in character and behaviour . . . an Aston. Imagine being at the lights alongside a driver who thought he was in a fast car and burning him up when the lights changed to green . . .

Johns was a large man, partly because of inherited characteristics, partly because his wife liked her cooking to be appreciated, and he took life calmly and quietly which sometimes led others to make the mistake of believing him of slow intelligence.

The ancient, gnarled oak tree grew inside the field and only the lower branches stretched out over the grass verge. The branch which had fallen had been pulled to one side, to clear the road, and he visually examined it. Normally, when a branch broke away from a trunk it was possible to judge why, but here all the wood looked perfectly healthy and there had been only a light wind in the latter part of the evening . . .

The grass verge was no more than a metre and a half wide at its widest. Impossible for a large car to mount it, roughly at right angles, to the point where the car was completely clear of the road. The ground was damp from all the recent rain; there was no impression of tyres. The boy had referred to a dry-stone wall. Although the majority of fields were bounded by dry-stone walls, sometimes topped with earth and stunted thorn hedges, here there was solely a thick thorn hedge. No car had recently hit that.

He put his hands in his pockets and jingled some coins that were in the right-hand one. Looking at things from a layman's point of view – one which might be upturned by medical evidence – it seemed impossible that the boy's memories could have had their origins in what had apparently actually happened. Surely, even if the blow had twisted his memory until that was false, there would at least have been one or two points at which it would have been possible to trace the pattern from the reality? For instance, a large tree which, in memory, shrank to a small tree. But here, virtually every detail was completely different.

He returned to his car and sat behind the wheel, but did not immediately drive away. In the CID they were so busy that any man who didn't do the work of two was shirking. So, unless it was clear that a crime had been committed, it was difficult to justify – and it had to be justified – time spent on an investigation. Yet the facts – if they were facts – were intriguing. So as soon as he could he'd contact all the local hospitals with casualty departments and he'd ask if any of them had treated a man who'd been in a car accident near Thorwick. And if it proved humanly possible to find a further spare moment, there were other enquiries which could be made . . .

By lunch-time Nick's headache had receded, until for much of the time he could forget it, and when Ben asked if he felt up to an afternoon's fishing, he didn't hesitate.

They drove the nine miles to a tarn owned by friends of the Ransomes. Very different from Steerson Tarn, most people would have deemed it a lake, but its name dated back to the distant past and so tarn it was always called. Almost half a mile long, and shaped like a cucumber, it lay in the middle of a wood which had never been replanted and which offered the higgledy-piggledy mixture of trees, some old and dying, some mature, some young and thrusting, which delighted a nature lover but offended a forester. On the south bank there was a boat-house, seemingly as ancient as some of the trees, and this housed a rowing boat which, luckily for those who used it, was relatively new and in good condition.

They launched the boat and rowed out to the centre of the tarn, where there were no surface weeds and the fitful sunshine sparkled the still water. Their total catch was two fish, both so small they were immediately returned, but it was an afternoon to be treasured and remembered for its serene, timeless peace.

On their return to Fawver Cottage they sat down to a Cumberland tea. Nick had just finished his third scone, topped with butter, raspberry jam and clotted cream, and had regretfully come to the conclusion that he couldn't eat

19

anything more, when the front doorbell rang. Ben left and went through to the hall.

Caroline began to clear the table, then stopped stacking plates. 'I don't recognise the voice,' she said. She held her head slightly on one side as she listened to the low murmur of voices.

Nick grinned. There were times when she reminded him of a chirpy robin, darting this way and that, determined to find out what was going on everywhere.

The voices died away and she resumed the stacking of the plates. 'Luke said he might drop in this evening, but it's rather early for him. And in any case, that can't have been his voice . . . Oh, well, as my mother used to say, wait long enough and you're bound to learn.' This was a strange philosophy for her to suggest since she could seldom find the patience equably to wait for any length of time. However, on this occasion she was not called upon to show patience because Ben returned to the room. 'Who is it?' she asked, as she put the plates on a tray.

'A detective who's come to have a word with Nick.'

She bridled. 'Oh, he has, has he? Did you tell him that Nick's been seriously injured . . .'

Ben smiled briefly. 'He knows and he's promised to be brief.' He turned to Nick. 'You're up to answering questions, aren't you?'

'Yes, of course.'

'Then come along through to the sitting-room.'

'I'm coming as well,' announced Caroline belligerently. 'And I'll make absolutely certain that he doesn't try to bully Nick.'

Ben winked at Nick. It would be a rash man indeed who tried to bully Nick while she was around to defend him!

Johns' quiet, friendly manner soon made it clear to Caroline that he'd no intention of bullying anyone. Indeed, after only a short time, she asked him whether he'd like a coffee and when he said he would, she hurried out of the room to make it.

Johns settled back in one of the armchairs – bright with

20

colour because Caroline believed life should be filled with colour – and said: 'The best thing, Nick, is if you'll tell me exactly what happened. I've heard some of it from other people, but now I want it straight from the horse's mouth. No insult intended!'

Nick described events from the moment he'd reached a T-junction and hadn't known which road to take . . . As he finished speaking, Caroline returned to the room with a cup of coffee, milk and sugar, on a small tray. Johns thanked her, added milk and two spoonfuls of sugar to the coffee, stirred vigorously, and drank. 'Lovely coffee,' he said. 'It's not often you get the real stuff these days, not with all the instant around.'

Caroline was gratified by his praise.

He spoke to Nick: 'How certain can you be that there wasn't a tree near the car?'

'Absolutely sure.'

'And you'd estimate the grass verge as something like five metres wide?'

'Something like that, yes. The car was at a bit of an angle, but its back was clear of the road.'

'Have you any idea what make of car it was?'

'That's difficult. I mean, seeing a shape in the fog and walking towards it and finding an injured man inside . . . I didn't really take in much about it except that it was green, and its registration letters which I noticed because they're the same as my initials.'

'Which are?'

'NAW.'

Johns made a quick note. 'What about the letter which gives the date – did you see what that was?'

'No, I didn't.'

'Would you reckon the car was a fairly recent model?'

'Almost brand new, judging by the smell; you know how a new car smells special?'

'I do – not that I've ever been able to afford one to enjoy it at first hand! Now, you said you don't know what make it was but suppose I asked you to make the best guess you could, what would you answer?'

Nick thought. 'One of the big Rovers. I seem to think the back window had that special slope to it.'

Johns wrote again. 'You thought the injured man was a foreigner?'

'He certainly looked like one, only . . . well, sometimes people who look like foreigners turn out not to be, don't they?'

'That's dead right.'

'But when he spoke, it wasn't in English.'

'And since he was obviously beginning to recover full consciousness, the odds must be that he was speaking in his native tongue. Any idea what language it was?'

'No. Except it wasn't French or Spanish and I'm ninety-nine per cent certain it wasn't German.'

'And then you heard something and began to turn and were knocked unconscious . . . Are you still certain that the sound came from behind you and not from above?'

'Yes, I am,' replied Nick, louder than was necessary.

'And you don't think it was like the noise a branch makes when it breaks away from its trunk?'

'I just told you, there wasn't a tree anywhere around.'

Johns smiled. 'I haven't forgotten. But it's my job to check up everything and anything. Can you describe the quality of the noise?'

'It was short and sharp and at the time I imagined it was a shoe hitting a stone. Then it was like the stone hitting something else.'

'About as far as you can get from a branch breaking free!' Johns stared down at his notebook for a moment, then shut this with a snap. 'That's the lot, then, and now I can get out from under your feet.'

Nick hesitated, then said: 'I promise I'm not making it all up.'

'Let's get one thing dead straight. There's not the slightest suggestion of that. It's a case of either your memory's been playing you some very funny tricks after that bash on the head

22

or else something pretty odd's been happening.'

'What d'you mean by odd?' asked Ben.

'Right now, Mr Ransome, I'd rather not try to answer that question. Maybe because I just have no idea what the answer is.' Johns smiled, but the expression in his eyes was calculating rather than amused.

Chapter 4

Detective Inspector Basdon looked to be a sour man, which was unfortunate because he was not; largely to blame was the scar which pulled down the right-hand corner of his mouth, a memento of a fight fifteen years before in which he'd nearly lost his life. He had a forthright manner and, in the face of incompetence, something of an explosive temper; those who worked under him respected him, but frequently wished that his standards were not so high.

He leaned back, rested his elbows on the arms of the chair, joined the fingers of his two hands at their tips, and stared at Johns above the triangle his forearms now made. 'You think the boy's memories are accurate?'

'After talking to him and Doctor Boshover, I'd say that they're just as likely to be accurate as inaccurate.'

'So how do you propose to find out which?'

'To begin with, I'd like to feed the registration letters through the computer and see if we can come up with a list of potential owners.'

'Bit of a long shot; or, rather, a hell of a long list.'

'Not necessarily.' Johns had long since learned that Basdon invariably homed in on any doubtful point or weakness in a case, thereby forcing the investigating officer to reconsider his work. 'Nick can't be certain, but he thinks it was a big Rover; youngsters usually know their cars. The inside smelled like a new car – at a guess that means something under six months old. It was green. So I'll ask the computer to spit out all green Rovers not more than six months old whose registration letters are NAW.'

'Even with those qualifications, it could still add up to a fairly large number of possibles.'

'But not too large to check.'

'If we didn't already have twice as much work in hand as we can reasonably cope with.'

There was a short silence, which Johns broke. 'All right, so far we've nothing to say definitely that any sort of crime was committed . . .'

'On the contrary. We've considerable evidence to suggest that none whatsoever has been.'

'But if there *was* a crashed car, if there *was* an injured man inside it, if Nick *was* deliberately knocked out, and if events *were* staged to make it look as if he'd been injured by a falling branch elsewhere . . . Then obviously something big has occurred, which someone needed to hush up.'

'What kind of something?'

Johns shrugged his broad shoulders.

Basdon spoke ironically. 'Normally, we're faced by a crime and we have to start searching out the facts which surround it; you want to reverse that sequence. You have the facts – only you can't be certain they are facts – and you're searching for the crime they surround.'

Johns said nothing.

'Have you checked with hospitals to see if one of them treated a man involved in a car crash near Thorwick?'

'None did.'

Basdon lowered his arms. He picked up a pencil from the desk and fiddled with it, rolling it between thumb and forefinger. 'Which, of course, you'd expect if Nick's memory is faulty.'

'Also what you'd expect, sir, if there's something which has to be hushed up so that no matter how badly injured the man was, he didn't dare attend a hospital.'

Basdon never made up his mind until satisfied he'd heard all the available evidence, then he made it up quickly and without reservations. 'Very well. Put the number to the computer. But I want to see what size the list of cars is before you take any further action.'

'Right, sir.' Johns turned and went over to the door.

'By the way, have you tried to trace the spot where Nick Wood claims to have seen the car?'

'Not yet.'

'Might be an idea to get on to that.'

It had been easy to follow the initial part of Nick's ride back from Steerson Tarn, but soon things became very much more complicated. The land was hilly and the roads and lanes numerous and serpentine. Remembering that he had been cycling in fog, when direction and distance became distorted, it soon became clear that he might have taken any one of four roads.

Johns drove down the first of these, his mind concentrated on the problem and not the view which spread out to his right; hills in the foreground, mountains in the background spearing up into the cloud-laden sky, their flanks green, their crests bare, defying the elements which inevitably must humble them. From what Nick had said, and remembering that he'd been pushing his bike from the time the fog closed in, it seemed he'd probably covered from two to four miles from the point at which his route might have been along any one of the four roads . . . When the odometer showed he'd covered five miles from that last reference, Johns stopped and used a farmyard in which to turn.

The second and third roads proved equally negative, but when two and two tenths miles down the fourth road he came up to a very sharp right-angled bend – lacking any warning sign – on the outer side of which was an unusually deep verge.

He parked the car and climbed out. The grass verge was heavily rutted, ostensibly by a succession of vehicles. Why? Here, the hills closed in so that there was no spectacular scene and tourists would not have used it as a viewing point. So had one car driven backwards and forward, to hid the ruts which had marked the passage of a single car?

The verge was bordered by a dry-stone wall. While almost the whole length of this was in a very good state of repair, there had been a fall at one point. Why? It was unusual for a wall this well-built to collapse from natural causes.

In the boot of his car was a pair of wellingtons and he changed into these. He crossed the muddy surface, avoiding the worst of the ruts, to the point at which the wall had fallen. Working quickly but, as he recognised, not very skilfully, he used the loose rocks to try to repair that section of the wall. He used up all of them before the repairs were complete. Had locals helped themselves to repair their own walls? But that was quite contrary to the way in which the normal farmer would act. Had the wall deliberately been wrecked so that some of the stones could be removed without this fact being immediately obvious – and had they been removed because they bore the scars of having been hit by a green car?

Nick had described how the nearside wing had been crumpled against the wall. The lights must have been smashed, which would have resulted in a litter of broken glass. Johns returned to his car for a rubber mat. He put this on the ground, knelt, and began to search. Fifteen minutes later, he had found one small sliver of glass, which he slipped into an envelope. The one sliver that had escaped a previous search; or a piece of glass which had never seen a car?

He changed back into his shoes and put the now muddy wellingtons and the wet rubber mat in the boot of his car. As he slammed the lid shut, he thought wryly that he had come to find answers, but he was leaving with no answers and many more questions.

The telephone rang and Detective Inspector Basdon looked at it with sharp dislike. But his dislike didn't stop it ringing. Finally, he reached out and lifted the receiver.

'This is Detective Superintendent Farr, Special Branch. I want to know why one of your men put through to the computer a search and advise on a car registration, numbers unknown, letters NAW.'

Basdon knew a sharp excitement. 'Then there is something in it!'

'What d'you mean by that?' The superintendent's abrupt

and sometimes discourteous manner often gave offence; he didn't care whom he offended.

'We've had reported a set of circumstances, sir, which could add up to something or could add up to nothing. If a large green car, possibly a Rover, almost new, registration letters NAW, was involved in an accident on Tuesday afternoon, then the odds are that something's brewing.'

'What are the circumstances?'

Briefly, Basdon reported the facts.

'He judged the injured man to be a foreigner?'

'Yes. He admits he could be wrong, but is adamant that the man spoke a foreign language when he was coming to.'

Farr said: 'I'm coming straight up by shuttle to Manchester. Send a car down to fetch me from there.'

Farr was due to retire in just under a year's time, a fact that both pleased and annoyed him. Pleased, because at long last he would be able to lead a life largely regulated by himself and not by outside forces; annoyed, because having held high rank he inevitably had begun to think of himself as indispensable and irreplaceable and it was not good for his *amour-propre* to have to face the fact that he was neither.

He was a large, well-built man who still took sufficient exercise so that clothes which had fitted him many years previously still did; indeed, since he was careless about his appearance, quite often his suit or casual clothes reflected that fact.

He paced Basdon's office, from the inside wall to the window, hands jammed into his pockets, square chin thrust slightly forward. There was more than a touch of John Bull about him. 'Did you know that your request for a computer search put a cat amongst the pigeons?'

'I didn't, no, not until you rang, sir. And I still don't know why.'

'Because Karim Sayyid ibn Ali owns a four months' old Rover, registration letters NAW.'

The name held no immediate significance for Basdon. He

28

wondered – since Farr's manner was so aggressive – whether Farr was deliberately trying to underline his ignorance. 'I don't recognise the name,' he said, accepting the challenge, if there was one.

Farr's expression briefly expressed approval. He liked men who stood up for themselves. 'Roughly six weeks ago, under the name of Karim Ali, he was charged with conspiring to deal in drugs.'

Basdon whistled.

'That's right. Only if you're to get things into perspective, you need to whistle a lot louder than that.' He crossed to the desk and sat down on a corner. 'Since your request to the computer, I've had an assistant commissioner on my back because he's had a high-up from the Foreign Office practically having hysterics on the phone.'

'How does the Foreign Office come into it?'

'If I knew the full answer to that, I'd be a happier man . . . Karim Ali holds an Iranian passport and according to him left Iran very shortly after the Shah – on his own admission, he was only one short jump ahead of the murdering mobs. He's very wealthy with no known job. His volunteered explanation of his wealth is that he brought a fortune in jewels out of Iran. As far as we're concerned, we knew nothing about him until he was arrested. His arrest followed a surveillance job on one of the top drug barons. Unfortunately, although the police team are quite certain he's up to his neck in the racket, he could only be charged with a relatively minor offence through lack of hard evidence. Obviously, the strong hope was that further evidence would be turned up later, but that hasn't happened so far. After his arrest, he was taken before magistrates and they, being a bunch of liberals who think the criminal is more important than the victim, released him on bail instead of keeping him locked up inside; they did, however, impose certain conditions of bail – he had to hand in his passport, report to the local police three times a week, and remain within ten miles of his home except with police permission.

29

'Since the magistrates' hearing, the Foreign Office has been under pressure from the Shishanna Embassy . . . What do you know about that country?'

'Next to nothing, I suppose, except it's down by Oman and it's got so much oil that the streets are paved with platinum.'

'I've heard it described as a land of sand, flies, and the biggest cut-throats in the Arabian Peninsula. That's as maybe, but since the discovery of oil, the sultan is certainly one of the richest men in the world. And even more to the point, pro-Western. When it seemed likely there was going to be a world oil shortage severe enough to cripple the industrialised nations, he stepped up production of oil. When Russia started putting pressure on him not to help the West, he refused to listen. The modernisation of his country has been carried out by Western nations – France, America, and most notably, Britain. I'm told that one contract alone, building the new airport, meant half a billion dollars to a consortium of British firms . . . And when I add that the Shishanna Embassy in London has concerned itself in Karim Ali's troubles to the extent of indicating very strongly that they'd like him to be dismissed from the case and that if he isn't, but is imprisoned, the Shishanna government – which means, of course, the sultan – will review their pro-Western, pro-British policies, you'll begin to understand why the Foreign Office is having kittens.'

'Why their concern, if Ali is an Iranian?'

'A good question. The simple answer is, we don't know. We can only surmise. Obviously, if Ali was close to the Shah, he can't appeal to his own embassy for help – they'd be delighted to see him jailed for life. So he must have scratched around until he found someone with enough clout who'd shout for him.'

'How d'you bribe one of the richest men in the world?'

'Another good question. Not with money, presumably. But if Ali escaped from Iran with jewels of unique quality, perhaps he used one or more of those; rich, powerful men often become compulsive collectors of things so valuable and rare that they reflect their wealth and power. Or maybe it isn't a case of bribery at all, but of returning favours granted when oil hadn't been found in Shishanna and it was merely a land of sand and flies.'

'What's been the reaction to the pressure?'

'Give the politicians and diplomats their due,' said Farr reluctantly, 'they've made it quite clear that in this country there can be no political control over the courts or the police. At the same time, it's obvious that if Ali's found not guilty at his trial and therefore escapes punishment, a lot of people in high-up places will be very relieved.'

'That's hypocritical.'

'What is politics but the exercise of hypocrisy?' Farr was silent for a while, then he spoke again. 'Now you'll understand why your request rang the alarm bells. And when you tell me that the man in the car had a leg in plaster, and I tell you that Karim Ali suffered a broken leg a fortnight ago, you'll also understand that those alarm bells are becoming deafening.'

Basdon said slowly: 'If there was that car accident and the injured man was Karim Ali, he'd have broken one of the conditions of his bail. He'd be jailed.'

'Which would precipitate the situation our government is desperate to avoid.'

'All the evidence so far points to the fact that Nick's memory has to be wrong. So do I accept that – and it would be very easy to justify doing so – and stop the investigations?'

'What would you do if I had not told you what I have?'

'Check further because my detective sergeant judges that we should.'

'Then you check further. But always remembering that if you decide it was Ali in the car and therefore he broke one of his bail conditions, you'll need overwhelming proof of the facts to justify your actions.'

'You're putting me in one hell of a position!'

'I'm not,' said Farr curtly, 'the circumstances are.'

Chapter 5

Manners Deep, originally Queen Anne, but refronted in Victorian times, was set in a park of almost one hundred acres. It was a large house, though not so large as to become overwhelming, and because the refronting had been carried out with sympathy for the original design its appearance was attractive.

As they approached the turning-circle, marked by a raised, circular flower-bed filled with colour at the end of the drive, Johns said to Basdon: 'This is the kind of place I'm going to have when I win the pools. And I'll employ a fat-jowled, ancient butler, who'll wear a black coat and striped trousers, who'll be extremely rude to any of my former colleagues who are presumptuous enough to try to use the front door . . .'

'Belt up.'

Basdon was in a state of nervous uncertainty, thought Johns, which was very unusual indeed. Just exactly what news had the detective superintendent from the Special Branch brought? . . . He braked to a halt, switched off the engine, released the safety belt, opened the door and climbed out. He looked up at the house. Here was a piece of history and it was a pity that they couldn't have recognised this by turning up in a coach and four . . .

'Are you intending to spend the rest of the day just standing there?'

He hurried into the elaborate porch and rang the bell, which was to the side of the large, studded, wooden door. After a very short wait the door was opened, not by a properly snooty butler but by a man slightly shorter than himself, and noticeably thinner, dressed in a jersey-shirt and green cotton trousers, whose speech identified him as a foreigner

32

far more readily than did his appearance.

He showed them into the library. A large, oblong room, it faced west and overlooked a part of the park in which grew a number of specimen trees. Much of the wall-space was shelves packed with leather-bound books; where the walls were bare, they had been panelled with oak. The room was dark, though not in the least gloomy. There were two desks, at opposite ends of the room, matching in style but not in size, several comfortable, leather-covered chairs and one chesterfield. On the parquet floor were two Persian prayer carpets of traditional design, alive with rich, subtle colours.

They heard the quick tap of shoes on a hard surface and turned to face the door. A woman entered. Of medium height, slim, she had a round, olive-complexioned face, immediately noticeable for its regularity and dark brown, lustrous eyes. She wore several pieces of jewellery and a dress that discreetly emphasised her figure. 'Good afternoon,' she said, in a voice that carried a hint of sing-song. 'My husband soon will come.' Her accent was heavy, but there was no trouble in understanding her.

'Sorry to interrupt you like this,' said Basdon with formal politeness, 'but the matter is important.'

'You like some coffee?'

'Thanks very much, but we had a mug just before we came out.'

'A drink?'

'Not right now, if it's all the same to you.'

Speak for yourself, Johns thought; then realised that Basdon had.

They heard an irregular thump of feet.

'Is husband now,' she said unnecessarily.

Karim Ali entered the room. Taller than she, but not as tall as either of the detectives, he wore a jacket whose every line proclaimed bespoke tailoring and a pair of old flannels, the right leg of which had been opened out to accommodate the plaster. His hair was jet black and showed signs of curliness; his cheekbones were high, his nose large and slightly hooked;

33

his moustache and beard were as black as his hair and very neatly trimmed so that they added to the picture of someone who took great care over his personal appearance. 'Good afternoon,' he said, his English very much more fluent than his wife's and not nearly so heavily accented. 'I understand from Farahnaz that you wish to speak with me?'

Both the detectives had studied his right cheek the moment he stepped into the library. It was unblemished. Remembering Nick's description of a deep, crescent-shaped cut and extensive surrounding bruising, it was obvious that Karim Ali had suffered no such injuries.

Basdon said, in a neutral tone: 'We've some questions we hope you won't mind answering.'

'I am delighted to give all the assistance I can. Then, perhaps, you will understand that to say I am a merchant in drugs is so ridiculous.'

'We aren't here on that account.'

'No?' He looked surprised. His wife spoke to him in Arabic. He answered briefly, turned to Basdon, and said in English: 'My wife wishes to know if she may leave as she has much to do.'

'Of course she may.'

He spoke to his wife and she left, carefully shutting the door after herself. 'You will understand,' he said, 'that after our experiences in Iran, we are still not used to the way in which in this country one remains free to do what one wishes even when the police are present . . . Please to sit down, gentlemen. And tell me what questions it is you wish to ask, if not about the unfortunate affair in Manchester which has been such a sad mistake.'

They sat. Basdon said: 'Under the terms of your bail, you are not permitted to travel more than ten miles from here except with the express permission of the police.'

'Unfortunately, that is so.'

'Have you on any occasion broken that condition?'

'But of course not.' Karim Ali gestured with his hands. 'Gentlemen, I am not a particularly wise man, but neither am

34

I a fool. When the court tells me I may not do this, even though they are so mistaken in their judgements, I most definitely do not do it.'

'Did you go out in your car on Tuesday?'

He thought. 'It is hard to be certain of one day from another, but I do not think I left the house then.'

'You didn't drive as far as Thorwick?'

'Thorwick? I think I do not know of such a place.'

'It's a small village, a couple of miles or so from Kirkstable.'

'But Kirkstable is many miles away.'

'About twenty.'

'Then I could not have gone there.'

'You could. The question is, did you?'

Karim Ali looked puzzled. 'Please? I do not fully understand.'

'Did you drive to Thorwick on Tuesday?'

'Of course I did not, it is so far away.'

'I believe you own a green Rover?'

'That is so.'

'Where is it now?'

He showed his surprise. 'In the garage, I trust. Should it be somewhere else?'

'Would you mind if we have a look at it?'

'Naturally not.'

'Then if we might do so now?' Basdon stood.

Karim Ali came to his feet quite quickly despite the leg in plaster. 'I hope you do not mind if I do not go also? I try to move as little as possible because of my infirmity.' He tapped his right leg. 'But I will tell Izzat to be with you . . . You will find the name amusing, I think?'

'Find it what?' The question was so unexpected that it left Basdon momentarily off balance.

'Amusing.'

'No, not at all.'

'But is that not what people shout often in the game of cricket?'

Johns smiled. 'That's howzat.'

'Of course! A tiny difference in pronouncing and a very big difference in meaning. Sometimes I truly despair of speaking the English an Englishman speaks.' He clumped his way over to an old-fashioned call-bell. 'Will you return after you look at my car and enjoy a drink with me?'

'Thanks very much, but no. We have to get straight back.'

Once again, this time more sourly, Johns reflected that if given the chance, he'd have answered differently.

The door opened and the man who'd shown the two detectives into the library stepped just inside and waited. Karim Ali spoke to him in Arabic, then half-turned. 'Gentlemen, Izzat will lead you. And if we do not meet again before you leave, it has been a great pleasure.'

'Goodbye,' said Basdon brusquely.

They left and followed Izzat through the lofty hall with its enormous open fireplace, above which was a circle of swords, and out to the drive. They walked round the side of the house and this brought them to a range of buildings, sited around a large courtyard.

There were four cars in the garage – a Rover, a Land Rover, a Granada, and much older than the other three, a Fiat.

Watched by Izzat, who did not once speak, they began their examination of the green Rover. The left wing showed no signs of damage or repairs and the shading of the paintwork was consistent no matter at what angle it was regarded; the lights were intact. Johns found an old sack and he knelt on this and used a pencil torch to examine the underneath of the wing. There were no distortions or signs of replacement.

They returned to their car and left. The drive rose slowly to a low brow and then descended equally slowly; they had topped the brow and were approaching the gates when Basdon said: 'Well?'

'He wasn't injured three days ago.'

'Obviously not. So a lot of people are going to breathe much easier when they read my report.'

'But . . .' Johns braked to a halt just past the gates as he waited for a van to pass before turning on to the road. 'But nevertheless, he had every reason to want to hide the fact he'd been in an accident, his description matches the one Nick gave, he's a foreigner, his right leg is in plaster, and his car is a green Rover with the registration letters NAW. What are the odds against anyone else also fitting all those points?'

'A thousand to one?' Basdon shrugged his shoulders. 'For all I know, a hundred times that.'

'Then how did all the facts come together in Nick's mind if he never actually experienced them?'

'Damned if I can answer. Unless he read about the preliminary hearing and the details stuck in his subconscious.'

'Ali hadn't broken his leg then.'

Basdon sighed. 'I'm just a copper, not a psychologist. I don't know how a person's mind can twist things. All I can be certain of is that since his face isn't scarred and bruised, and his Rover is equally unmarked, Ali couldn't have been in any accident.'

On Saturday morning, Nick went to Keswick with Caroline and while she shopped he wandered around the town, enjoying a block of mint cake as he did so. He met her back in the car park. 'It's not very late, Nick, so we've time to return by the long route. You wouldn't mind that, would you?'

'I'd like it.'

'Good. On a sunny day like this, it's such a beautiful run. And so very different from when the weather's foul and we can't think why we don't move and live somewhere where it rains for only half the year.'

They left Keswick a little before twelve and arrived back at Fawver Cottage at ten to one. A car was parked outside the front gate. 'Now who on earth's that?' she said, a touch of annoyance in her voice. 'Well, whoever it is, I have to get lunch. I'll bet you're starving.'

'I'm not really all that hungry.'

She turned to look at him. 'You are feeling all right?'

'Perfectly. It's just that I had some mint cake in Keswick.'

She laughed. 'So much for my sudden worries . . . When I

37

was your age, my biggest treat was mint cake, but now I find it too sweet. One of the penalties of growing old!'

Carrying most of the shopping, he followed her into the house and, as soon as they were inside and heard the voices in the sitting-room, they identified their visitor as Detective Sergeant Johns.

'Just dump the stuff in the kitchen, Nick, and then go on through.'

Nick put the two bags of shopping on the kitchen table, made his way through to the sitting-room.

'You're finally back!' said Ben. 'I told the sergeant you'd probably be here by half twelve.'

'We came by the back route.'

'Should have thought of that, on a day like this.'

Johns said in his deep, occasionally lazy voice: 'There's no need to worry on my account.' He held up a pewter tankard. 'With some of the local brew to hand, waiting's a pleasure. You're looking a lot fitter, Nick.'

'I'm right back to normal.'

'Is that a good or a bad thing?' asked Ben.

Johns laughed. Nick said eagerly: 'Have you been able to find out about the car?'

'As I was telling Mr Ransome earlier, we've been checking up on what you told us as hard as we could. Cutting a long story short, we've identified a foreigner who owns a new green Rover with the registration letters NAW, who had good reason to hide the fact he'd been in a car crash in Thorwick, and whose right leg's in plaster.'

'Then you've proved I wasn't dreaming?'

Johns shook his head. 'We interviewed him and examined his Rover. He's not received any recent injury to his right cheek and his Rover has not been in an accident.'

Nick showed both his disappointment and growing bewilderment.

'Does he resemble Nick's description?' Ben asked.

'Yes.'

'Then what's the explanation?'

'That's what's brought me here, Mr Ransome.' Johns turned to Nick. 'Do you read the newpapers regularly?'

'Normally, yes.'

'Do you recall about six weeks ago reading a case in which a man who lives not all that far from here appeared before magistrates in Manchester on a charge of conspiring to deal in drugs?'

'I don't think so, no.'

'Will it help if I add that he was granted bail on condition he surrendered his passport, didn't travel more than ten miles from his home, and reported three times a week to his local police?'

'I certainly don't remember anything like that.'

Ben said: 'Are you wondering if Nick had read about the case and stored the details in his subconscious and the blow on the head released them to form a false memory?'

'Something along those lines.'

'Did the newspaper reports give the registration letters of the Rover?'

'I doubt it.'

'Then how could Nick have remembered them?'

'Nick told me he noticed the letters because they were the same as his initials; perhaps his memory transferred his initials to the car's registration.'

'Which coincidentally happened to be the letters of the Rover of a possible suspect? Wouldn't you call that a remarkable coincidence?'

'Yes,' admitted Johns.

'And isn't it an equally remarkable coincidence that the possible suspect resembles the person Nick described?'

'That's more easily explained – his photograph may have been published. And come to that, of course, he might have been by his car . . .' He shrugged his shoulders. 'Look, I know it all sounds difficult. But if you accept that it can't have been this man, then you have to find some other explanation. And the only alternative, as I see it, to Nick's memory having worked in strange ways is that there's another Rover with those registration letters, owned by a foreigner who's recently broken his leg, who had a good reason to conceal the crash.'

'So you're choosing the easier option?'

'That's not fair, Mr Ransome; we're checking out all other possible owners to cover the wildest of coincidences.'

'I suppose I was being unfair. It's just that, not being a neurologist or psychologist, I find it very difficult to believe that anyone can have so clear a memory of a sequence of events if they were all imaginary.'

'I'd have gone along with that until now.'

'But you're convinced that that's what happened?'

'Unless we find another Rover owner who fits the bill, yes.' Johns lifted up the tankard and drained it. He stood. 'One last thing, Nick. Just let me repeat – we're convinced that everything you've told us has been said in the best of faith; if you've been wrong, it's in no way your fault.'

'At least that's something.' For the first time, Nick began seriously to know some self-doubt.

Chapter 6

Nick rang home just before lunch on Sunday.

'Are you enjoying yourself?' Thelma asked.

'Very much, Mum. And tomorrow if it's fine and not windy, Uncle Ben's taking me to Windermere where a friend of his will take me out water-skiing.'

'You will be careful, won't you?'

'Of course I will. Especially after Tuesday.'

'What d'you mean by that?'

'I had a bit of a thump on the head, but there's no panic because I didn't get concussion and now everything's back to normal.'

'How on earth did that happen?'

'Someone hit me or a branch fell on me.'

'For goodness sake, you must know which.'

'Not really. You see . . .' He told her what had happened.

Her reaction was predictable. 'Why didn't Caroline ring immediately and tell me?'

'She asked whether I thought she should and I said not. I mean, I was quite all right and if you'd known then, you'd only have fussed.'

'I don't call it fussing to worry if one's son is badly injured.'

'I wasn't badly injured and I'm fine now.'

She hesitated, then her resentment not gone, said 'Are you sure you really are fit?'

'Firing on all twelve cylinders.'

'I suppose in that case . . .' She latched on to something on which she could vent her annoyance. 'Why wouldn't the police believe you? They've no right to disbelieve anything you say.'

He wondered if he could remind her of those words the next

41

time she refused to accept some ingenious excuse of his. 'Mum, they're not calling me a liar . . .'

'I should certainly hope they are not.'

'They're just saying that the blow on my head sent my memory into a spin.'

'Ridiculous!'

'I know it sounds screwy, but they've checked and checked and I can't have been right.'

'Then they haven't checked enough . . .'

After a while, he interrupted her to say that he thought he ought to ring off because it had been rather a long call.

'Have you seen the doctor yet today?'

'There's been no reason to.'

'And how do *you* know that?'

'Because the quack told me on Tuesday that if I didn't start seeing double or heaving up, I was all right.'

She was silent for a moment, then she said, in tones of sorrowful doubt: 'I just hope he's right . . . You're to get in touch with me immediately if anything, anything at all, happens. Do you understand?'

'All right. Provided I don't die first.'

'That is not in the least bit funny . . . Give my love to Caroline, but tell her . . . I suppose you'd better not.'

After saying goodbye, Nick replaced the receiver. Poor Mum, he thought; she'd spend the rest of the day thinking up all the possible long-term effects of a heavy blow to the head. Still, Dad would eventually make her laugh at her own fears . . .

Perhaps it was time he learned to laugh at himself. All right, the memories seemed too sharply defined to be false, yet the facts said that they had to be. So accept that he'd appeared to live through a dramatic event when he hadn't. It didn't mean he was beginning to go off his rocker, it just proved that he had a very vivid imagination. What a pity the memory hadn't been of meeting someone with a Vantage Aston who'd taken him for a drive and touched a hundred and forty. He grinned. But how frustrating to have to accept the fact that nothing of

42

the sort had actually happened to him!

Monday started off overcast, but then the light westerly wind slowly harried the clouds until the day became reasonably sunny.

Nick had previously done enough water-skiing to be fairly proficient at it, but he soon discovered muscles he had not used for a long time; by the middle of the afternoon he was glad to stop. They drove back to Stillthwaite soon afterwards and when he walked into the sitting-room of Fawver Cottage it was to discover that a visitor had called to see him. 'Judy!' he exclaimed in loud amazement, as he stared at his cousin. 'What in the world are you doing here?'

'What d'you think? I wanted to see how you were after your accident.'

'You don't mean to say you've come up from London just for that?'

'Why not? After all, you are my very favourite cousin.'

Caroline was surprised; had she been asked, she'd have judged that Judy was not the kind of person to put herself out for anyone. Ben, less cynical, thought that Judy, with her naturally curly, blonde hair, deep blue eyes, and a figure that promised near perfection, was one of the most attractive girls he'd seen for a long time.

'How did you know I'd had an accident?' Nick asked.

'Mother telephoned Uncle Patrick last night and he told her. When I heard, I said I simply had to come up and see for myself that you really were all right.'

'Didn't Dad tell your mum that I was?'

'Of course he did, but I reckoned you might be belittling everything in order to stop Aunt Thelma worrying too much.'

'But . . .' He came to a stop. He was very fond of Judy – except when in one of her superior moments – but this did seem to him out of character. As Caroline had surmised – not that he was aware of this – Judy normally did not concern herself overmuch with other people's problems.

'Surely you're glad I'm here?' She sounded a little hurt.

43

If she really had made the journey specially, it was obviously churlish of him not to show his appreciation. 'Of course I am – a hundred and one per cent glad. It's just that I was surprised.'

'Nicely, I hope?'

'That is a different question!'

She laughed, a wide, happy laugh that made her look far less sophisticated. 'Now I know you're right back to normal!'

Caroline said: 'How about some tea?'

'Yes, please,' replied Nick immediately.

'I've cooked some more of those scones you like . . . Judy, do you like scones?'

'I love them, but really I shouldn't eat them.'

'Why ever not?'

'I have to think of my figure.'

'These days, you youngsters spend far too much time thinking about your figures,' said Caroline brusquely. 'Do you prefer tea or coffee?'

'I like whatever anyone else has.'

'Coffee. Right, I'll go out and prepare things.'

'And I guess I'd better check whether the greenhouse needs watering,' said Ben.

After the other two had left, Nick said to Judy, whose print dress fortuitously went so well with the loose-cover of the armchair she was sitting in: 'Where are you staying?'

'With friends, who've a house just outside Keir Brook.'

'Keir Brook. Isn't that less than four miles away?'

'Something like that. It had to be near, didn't it, if it was to be easy to get over to see you?'

'No kidding, you really did come up just to see how I was?'

'How many more times have I got to tell you, yes?'

'It's great of you,' he said warmly.

It was nearly half-past six when Judy said: 'I think I ought to start on my way back.'

'If it's so close, I'll come with you,' said Nick.

'That would be great.' She paused, then added: 'If you're

44

sure you're not too tired after all that water-skiing?'

'Of course not.'

She was the perfect guest. She thanked Caroline for the wonderful tea, said she'd never before had such delicious scones, and hoped she'd see both Caroline and Ben again.

Ben saw them leave on bicycles, then returned indoors to the kitchen where Caroline had begun washing up.

'Charming girl!' he said enthusiastically, as he picked up a tea-towel. 'So good-mannered compared to some these days.'

Caroline smiled as she transferred some glasses from the rinsing bowl to the draining-board.

Chapter 7

As they left Stillthwaite, Judy said something which Nick failed to hear. Since the road was empty of other traffic and for the moment straight, he increased his rate of pedalling to draw level. 'What was that?'

'I said, I've been thinking.'

'That'll help the world go round!'

'A lot more than if ever you tried it . . . I've been thinking about your hallucination.'

'I did not have a hallucination.'

'Yes, you did, if you thought you saw a whole series of external objects which weren't actually there. Only I wonder if you . . .'

'If you think I made it all up –'

'I know you can't have done.'

'What makes you that certain?'

'You'd never think up something which left you looking a bit stupid.'

He slowed and she drew ahead. She might be very attractive, she might have made a long journey especially to see he was fit again, but her tongue remained too sharp for everyone's good.

She briefly looked back. 'I haven't annoyed you, have I?'

'Of course not,' he answered loftily. He was not so small-minded that a casual, illogical, and ridiculous observation could in the slightest degree upset him.

She slowed before he realised what was happening, so that they were once more abreast. 'Tell me something, Nick. Is your memory of what happened a bit blurred around the edges?'

'No.'

'So you remember everything clearly?'

'So clearly that after I'd described the place where I saw the car, the police were able to find it.'

'With what result?'

'They discovered a sliver of glass which might have come from a crushed headlamp and they think it's possible some stones are missing from the dry-stone wall.'

'What's the significance of them?'

'When a car crashes into something, inevitably part of the car's paint becomes impacted on to that something and it can be next to impossible to remove all traces so that the police scientists can't find them. So if you wanted to hide what had happened, you'd take away any rocks which bore scars or paint. And to hide the fact that you'd taken 'em, you'd make it look as if the wall had fallen down a bit.'

'You do know a lot of things!'

Honesty made him admit: 'I only know all that because the detective sergeant told me.'

'I'm sure that's not wholly true . . . If they found all that, why are they so certain you can't have lived your memory?'

'Because they checked out all new green Rovers with the registration letters I saw and only one of them belongs to a foreigner who fits my description, whose leg is in plaster, and who has a reason for hiding the incident.'

'Why can't it have been he who was in the car?'

'There was no cut or bruising on his cheek and there's no way that that could have disappeared in three days. On top of that, his Rover's never been in any sort of a crash.'

'But how could you have imagined seeing someone exactly like him?'

'He was up in court a few weeks back. I must have read about him and seen a photo of him and stored the facts in my brain without ever realising it.'

'Do you think that that's what happened?'

'I don't know what to think, except . . . if the facts say I can't actually have seen him, then I can't.'

'I wonder.' She pedalled on for twenty metres, then said:

'From your point of view, everything depends on how much confidence you have in yourself. And, of course, there's the corollary, how much are you prepared to let other people manipulate your thoughts?'

'What's all that supposed to mean?'

'That you ought to learn to stand up for yourself.'

'Thanks very much. After being bashed unconscious and having a headache that felt as if a man was working away inside my skull with a pneumatic drill . . .'

'You only confuse things by being melodramatic.'

'I can just about begin to imagine how melodramatic you'd have got if all this had happened to you! And why are you going on and on about it when it's over and done with? . . . Hey! I'm beginning to understand something.'

'Congratulations on a rare event.'

'You didn't come up here because you were worried how I was.'

'I certainly did. And it's very, very ungrateful of you . . .'

'You came because you thought there might be some excitement going and you didn't want to be left out of it.'

'This is the last time that I'll be stupid enough to allow my good nature . . .'

'Your good nature never starts working until it's checked first what you want.'

'You are being very unkind,' she said, in a small, hurt voice.

'It's a wonder you don't start calling it the unkindest cut of all,' he said sarcastically.

'If I'd wanted to quote, I'd have quoted correctly and said "the most unkindest cut of all",' she replied, unable to resist her penchant for correcting inaccuracies.

There was a brief moment and them they both laughed, caught up in the humour of their bickering.

'Come on,' he said, 'tell the truth and shame the devil. You did come up because you wanted to know what was going on, didn't you?'

' " . . . tell the truth, and shame the devil!" . . . Maybe partly. But really it was mainly because I *was* so worried about you after that phone call from Uncle Patrick.'

She'd spoken so sincerely that he found it very difficult to disbelieve her.

They rounded a bend and this brought them to a hill. She dropped down to bottom gear and pedalled hard for a while, but then she stopped, climbed off, and began to walk. Not willing to appear to be boasting, he did the same, while assuring himself that he could have gone straight up to the top in *Tour-de-France* style if he'd been on his own.

As they climbed the view opened up; short, sharp hills, rocky outcrops, in the middle ground an abandoned slate mine, and in the background a bonfire which sent a thick column of smoke up into the air where it gradually spread out to the east.

'You're not in a hurry to get back, are you, Nick?'

'No. Why d'you ask?'

'Let's sit down and just enjoy the scenery for a bit. It's so different from home.'

'Since you live in the centre of London, that sounds logical.'

'You know perfectly well what I mean.'

They had reached a point where the land temporarily levelled out before rising a further sixty-five metres to the brow. They laid their bikes down, then settled near a rock which, as she pointed out, offered one profile which looked exactly like a Red Indian complete with head-dress. From far off they heard the haunting cry of a curlew.

She raised her knees and rested her chin on them, her hands linked together. 'Nick, be absolutely honest and forget everything the police have told you. Do you believe your memory is false?'

'But how can I forget all the evidence they've uncovered . . .'

'Just forget it!'

He reached out and picked a stem of grass which he began to chew. 'All right. I still think that what I remember probably happened.' Partly, he thought, because he didn't like to acknowledge that his mind had flipped.

'Then anything which proves it can't have done, has to be wrong.'

'Twist things round like that and yes, it does. But . . .'

'Forget all the buts. What seems to prove your memory must be wrong? The fact that the man with the leg in plaster doesn't have a cut and bruised cheek and that his Rover has never been in a crash. Let's start with the Rover. It's easy enough to go out and buy another newish green one that's undamaged and then change the registration plates over. And with the police so certain you had to be wrong, I'll bet they never checked that the engine and chassis numbers were the correct ones. So that takes care of the Rover.'

'Just like that!' But, he thought, it was possible. 'You can't just change cheeks, though.'

'You can change the man behind the cheek.'

'What on earth are you getting at now?'

'Look, I know at first sight the idea sounds far-fetched. But, as with so many things, the question of far-fetchedness depends on one's starting point. Start from the police's and it's too far-fetched for serious consideration; start from yours, and it's obvious that it's the only possible and logical explanation of what happened.'

'Possible and logical? Impossible and illogical.'

'Start thinking, instead of reacting like one of Pavlov's dogs.'

'Barking and biting?'

'Idiot!' she said good humouredly. 'Accept that you were right, then clearly someone went to an awful lot of trouble to make everyone think that you must be wrong. If they'll go to that much trouble, they'll go to a whole lot more and that includes impersonation.'

'You can't impersonate as easily as you're making out.'

'If you start with two men who naturally look alike and then get experts to help, you can, particularly when a moustache and beard cover up a large part of the face. And you're forgetting something very important.'

'I wouldn't be me if I didn't.'

50

'Nick, I'm not trying to jeer at you. It's just that you've been in the centre of everything and so it's impossible for you to step on one side and look at events with a fresh eye. But I can, especially when I know you well enough to be certain that when you say that if it weren't for the police's evidence you'd still believe in your memory, that your memory needs to be believed . . . The important thing you're forgetting is this. It's a recognised fact that all of us tend to see what we expect to see.'

'What's so important about that?'

'This. That the police visited a house they knew belonged to a possible suspect. If they were let in by someone who ac-knowledged the man as the owner – say, by a woman who claimed to be his wife – then they'll automatically have ac-cepted him as the person they'd come to see. And if any dissimilarities were noticed, perhaps from a photograph, these will have been put down to the fault of the photograph rather than the fault of the man.'

'The police must have thought about all this.'

'Don't you see, they don't have to consider this until they're convinced your version of events is the correct one. And they never have been, have they?'

'Just the opposite.'

'Precisely. So they won't have considered the possibility that the man they met was not the owner of the house and not the husband of the woman. And the fact that his cheek was unmarked, and his Rover was undamaged, confirmed them in their belief that you had to be wrong; and the more this was confirmed, the more they accepted his identity.'

'I must say . . .' he threw away the piece of grass he'd been chewing and picked another, 'you do make it all sound pos-sible.'

'Probable.'

'Suppose you're right . . .'

'Then obviously we start proving that.'

'We tell the police?'

'For heaven's sake, don't be so wet. They haven't believed

you so far, why on earth should they start now?'

'Because I'll finally be able to persuade them.'

'Pigs might fly,' she said crossly. While she had not exactly been lying when she said she'd come up from London to see how he was, had she been completely honest she would have added that a more pressing reason had been her hope that the journey would lead to some excitement.

Chapter 8

Johns walked into the detective inspector's office to find that Basdon was speaking on the telephone. He waited. Basdon replaced the receiver. 'I wonder why, that even after twenty-one years of marriage, one's wife still doesn't appreciate that there are times when one simply does, at the last moment, have to cry off from returning home to lunch . . . You're not married, are you?'

'Not yet.'

'If you want my advice . . . but when did the young ever want advice?' He leaned back in his chair.

'I've just had Nick Wood and his cousin in to see me, sir.'

'What's his problem this time?'

'It's more his cousin's really. She's quite some girl!'

'And from the enthusiasm, pretty?'

'A real smasher, but still young,' said Johns regretfully. 'Anyway, she's been giving me a lecture on logic and simple psychology.'

'I've a cousin like that. But she lives right down in Devon, thank goodness.'

'The gist of her lecture was this. Nick's memory is perfectly correct, so therefore some of the facts are wrong. We will only accept the logic of this when we remember that it's a well-known fact that a person tends to see what he expects to see.'

'She really went on like that?'

'Yes. But charmingly.' Johns gave a brief résumé of all that Judy and Nick had said.

Basdon spent a couple of seconds rubbing his back against the chair to quieten a sudden itch. 'How did you answer all that?'

'As tactfully as possible. I explained that we'd made a very full investigation and this had led us to the conclusion that his memory could not be right, but that such a conclusion wasn't either a direct or an implied criticism of him.'

'How was that received?'

'As a matter of fact, I found that a bit odd. She'd been going on so earnestly I expected her to argue, but she didn't. Then Nick asked who the man we'd identified and questioned was . . . I may be being a bit fanciful now, but I'd half an idea they'd thought of going and seeing Karim Ali for themselves.'

'You didn't name him?'

'Of course not, sir.'

'Then that's that?' It was a question as much as a statement.

Johns shifted his weight from one foot to another. 'I've got to admit, she did cause me to think over things again.'

'Obviously either her logic or her attraction was remarkable.'

Johns smiled wryly. 'A bit of both, maybe . . . You know, sir, she was right to this extent. If you do accept Nick's version of events, then some of the evidence has to be wrong.'

'But if the evidence is right, it's his version which has to be wrong. Remembering he'd had a pretty nasty blow on the head, which is the more likely?'

'I know, but . . . frankly, I've been wondering if we shouldn't go over everything just once more.'

Basdon sighed as he looked down at the numerous files and papers on his desk. 'We haven't the time to investigate properly all the incidents we know are criminal; do you really think we're justified in further diverting manpower away from them to investigate one incident which, all the evidence so far adduced suggests, was not criminal?'

'And a lot of people in high places will be much happier if it isn't proved that Karim Ali broke one of the conditions of his bail.'

'That consideration does not enter into it,' snapped Basdon angrily.

Didn't it? wondered Johns.

'I told you it would be a waste of time,' said Judy, as they walked away from the modern concrete-and-glass divisional HQ building.

'I still say we had to go and see them,' replied Nick.

'All right, we've done all the right and proper things and a fat distance it's taken us. So now we can –'

'Forget it all.'

'– see the man and prove he isn't who he says he is . . . Let's find somewhere where we can have a milk-shake and a think.'

'Milk being good for the brain?'

'A chocolate malted milk being something I adore. And I'll bet you'll not turn one down.'

That, he thought, was the safest of bets.

They turned into a side road and this brought them to the high street. Athrington was a small market town which had escaped most of the development which had overtaken and overpowered so many places up and down the country and its wide, tree-lined, main street still had an air of past times and gracious living about it; only a couple of recently built chain-stores introduced an unwelcome touch of contemporary values.

They found a café, run by Italians, and went in. Their choice, although fortuitous, was a good one. The ice-cream was supplied by a small manufacturer who produced quality rather than quantity.

They finished their first milk-shakes quickly. Judy stared down at her now empty glass, its sides streaked with milk foam, and said that it was a well-known fact that a second milk-shake always tasted better than the first one; she was going to order two more. Nick began to argue, very conscious of the fact that he couldn't really afford a second one, but she ignored his protests after the brief observation that her mother had given her extra pocket-money to spend up in Cumberland (like Ben, she refused to use the name Cumbria). He relaxed.

If he had Judy's pocket-money, let alone this extra, he'd be on the way to being able to buy that Aston Martin . . .

Halfway through the second milk-shake, she put the two straws down and looked directly at him. 'You know what we've got to do now, don't you?'

'If you mean about the car crash and all that, yes. Forget it.'

She spoke scornfully. 'What's got you running scared?'

'I am not.'

'Then why are you so funkery?'

'I'm realistic and prudent.'

'My eye!'

'Look, if the police won't do anything, there's nothing we can . . .'

'You saw the man in the car, they didn't. So you can identify the man in the house as an imposter, they can't.'

'But . . .'

'You told me the man never opened his eyes and wasn't really compos, so he can't have any idea of who you really are. We'll think up a good reason for calling and it'll be as easy as wink.'

'But . . .'

'You produce enough buts for *The Guinness Book of Records*. Don't you want to prove to the police that in fact you're not really missing a bit upstairs?'

'They've never thought I am.'

'Maybe they've not put it into so many words . . . But didn't you notice how Detective Sergeant Johns looked at you once or twice back at the police station?'

'What are you getting at?'

'He was laughing at you.'

'He certainly was not.'

'Nick, how d'you expect him to react when he believes you suffered hallucinations because a branch fell on to your head.'

'A branch did not fall on to my head. There wasn't a tree in sight . . .' At least, in his memory there hadn't been . . .

'There's no need to shout. I know all that, which is why I'm not laughing at you. But he doesn't, which is why he is . . . I must say, I'm surprised you don't want to prove yourself. I always thought you were someone with some self-respect.'

It was extraordinary, he thought, how she was two people; someone who was fun and great company and someone to whom it would have been a pleasure to say goodbye. Just because he recognised that common sense said there was nothing more they could or should do, he wasn't being so weak he wouldn't stand up for himself . . . Then he remembered something. She'd obviously overlooked one vital fact. He laughed to himself, because it wasn't often she gave him the chance to get the better of her. 'All right, then, we'll check the bloke out.'

'That's better! I knew you weren't really the kind of person who'd run away instead of fighting.'

She'd spoken with such sincerity that it was difficult to recall that less than a minute before she'd been suggesting that he was just such a person . . . 'I'll go and see him . . .'

She quickly interrupted. 'We'll go and see him.'

'Then we'll go and see him,' he agreed carelessly. 'And since I can remember what the man in the car looked like as clearly as if it all happened earlier this morning, I'll know immediately . . .' He came to a sudden stop.

'What's the matter?'

'We're forgetting something. We just can't do it.'

'Why not?'

'Mr Johns didn't tell us who the man is. Blast!' He tried to look thoroughly crestfallen.

'That's no problem,' she said airily.

'But if we've no idea who he is or where he lives . . .'

'You told me that Mr Johns said once that he lived reasonably locally, didn't you?'

'But that could mean anything from a couple of miles to fifty. Goodness only knows how many people live in that kind of an area and if you're thinking of getting in touch with every foreigner amongst 'em . . .'

'Some six weeks ago, he was up in a court in Manchester on a drugs charge. He was released on bail, on certain conditions.

There are bound to have been reports of the hearing in the national papers and more than likely, since he lives not far from here, in the local ones as well. The reports will identify him and may even give his address.'

It was suddenly obvious to him that she had thought all this out from the beginning. So when he'd agreed to her idea with such enthusiasm, thinking he was being very clever, she'd been laughing at him. Talk about being hoist with one's own petard! His sense of annoyance and disgruntlement slowly faded. It would be fun to carry out their own investigation and prove to the police that they were wrong . . .

It needed all of Judy's charm to gain permission to search through back copies of the *Athrington Gazette*, but finally she succeeded. They were led down a couple of corridors to a room smelling of dust and disuse, which was lined with large shelves on which were stored bound copies of the *Gazette*, dating back to the turn of the century when the first issue had appeared.

There was no difficulty in finding what they sought. The *Gazette* was a weekly newspaper and the hearing had obviously taken place in a week in which news items of greater importance had been lacking. They read the two columns of print. Karim Sayyid ibn Ali, an Iranian who had managed to escape from his country very soon after the Shah had abdicated, had appeared before magistrates in Manchester on a charge of conspiracy to deal in drugs. Karim Ali was a well known and respected owner of one of the county's historical estates, in Mealbeck; he was an ardent supporter of the Tillsman Hunt who met at his home, Manners Deep, twice a season. Commenting on the charge, he had told the reporter from the *Gazette* that it was all a terrible mistake and his lawyers would very soon be able to supply proof to that effect . . .

Chapter 9

Despite the closure over the years of so many branch lines, there was still a rail service between Keir Brook and Mealbeck and Judy and Nick, taking their bicycles with them, caught the eleven-fifteen train. This arrived at Mealbeck a couple of minutes before twelve, after a slow journey through largely unspoilt and beautiful countryside.

Only four other passengers disembarked and, after they had passed through the barrier, the ticket-collector had plenty of time to talk. A tall man, with bowed shoulders and the tanned, lined face of someone who'd spent much of his life in the open, he spoke with so thick an accent that both of them had to concentrate really hard to understand him. 'Manners Deep? Belongs to that A-rab.' He stretched out 'Arab' until it sounded like two words. 'Seen him here more'n once, when he's gone to Keswick. Quicker'n going by car.' He scratched the back of his neck. 'Been in trouble, so I been told. Wouldn't know about that. I takes people as I finds 'em. Always pleasant enough to me.' There was something about his tone of voice which suggested that the friendliness had had a financial basis. 'You'd be friends of his, would you?'

'Not directly,' replied Judy. 'But we know someone who suggested we call in and saw him if we were in this part of the world.'

'Oh, aye.'

'Can you tell us how to get to his place?'

'I reckon.' He scratched his neck again, then stared intently across the track at something.

She tried to conceal her impatience. 'Is it up the road, there?'

'That it ain't,' he said. It was impossible to judge from his lugubrious expression whether or not he was deliberately being irritatingly slow.

'Then which way is it?'

He slowly turned, pointed to his left. 'You goes up there for maybe two miles and you comes to crossroads. You turns right and comes to the house. Can't miss it. Big gates.' He scuffed his right shoe along the ground. 'I minds when Sir Percy lived there. Weren't safe to be on that road on account of him coming out of the park when he wanted and be dammed to anyone else.' He spoke with approval. A man of property should have the fire to act like a man of property . . .

They left the station, cycling slowly because the day was sunny and warm and there was no return train until four. At the crossroads they turned right and soon the road ran through a plantation of conifers, gloomy in their regimentation. Nick broke a silence which had lasted for several minutes. 'We'd better start looking out for somewhere to eat.'

'We're not eating until we've been to the house.'

He flexed his shoulders to realign slightly the straps of the backpack which held their lunch. 'I'm pretty hungry and . . .'

'Have you ever tried to think of something other than food?'

He had been going to add that there was something about setting out on a picnic which always made him extra hungry even before normal eating hours, but he checked the words. If she was in one of her vinegary moods, it was easier not to argue with her. Even at the expense of starving.

The trees stopped and open fields took their place. Half a mile further on they came to the park, marked by a high brick wall in very good repair. The main gateway was some way along. The large, wrought-iron gates were made to a complicated and slightly fussy design; to the left of them was an octagonal gate-house.

They cycled through the gateway and up the drive and, as they approached the brow of this, the house came into view, segment by segment.

'Quite some place!' said Nick admiringly.

'Isn't it? I wonder how long the estate was in the hands of the family of the previous owner.' Judy spoke thoughtfully. 'It must be awful if your family's owned a place like this for centuries and then you're forced to give it up. I'm sure Tennyson was wrong.'

'Couldn't agree more, but what's he to do with anything?'

'Haven't you ever read his *In Memoriam?*'

'Think I'm nuts?'

''Tis better to have loved and lost Than never to have loved at all . . . I'm certain it isn't. What you haven't had, you probably don't miss; or certainly not as much as if you have had it. Just imagine this being your home and then having to leave it. Think of all the bitter memories you'd have. You'd never be able to come within miles of here again.'

'I don't suppose it would be all that bad after a time.'

'When part of you's been wrenched away? Because our past is part and parcel of us, you know.'

When he thought about it in those terms, he supposed that the loss would always hurt . . . There were times when he was surprised by, and rather envious of, the width and depth of her mind. He knew very well that had he been on his own he would briefly have admired the house and grounds and envied the person rich enough to own them, but he would not have considered the feelings of the previous owner, forced out of possession of his past by a taxation system which – as his father frequently bore witness – was dedicated to ruining everyone.

They coasted down to the turning-circle and leant their bikes against the raised flower-bed. They crossed into the high, deep porch and he pulled the elaborate wrought-iron bell handle.

'I'm glad you're here,' she said in a low voice. 'I'd be terribly nervous on my own.'

He immediately felt taller.

The heavy wooden door was opened by a man of medium height whose cheeks were badly scarred from acne. When

Nick asked him if Mr Ali was in he replied in heavily accented English, his manner antagonistic rather than welcoming: 'Why you want?'

'We'd rather like a word with him, if that's possible.'

The man said nothing and remained motionless, staring at them. From inside, a woman called out in a language which neither Judy nor Nick could immediately identify. The man answered, the woman spoke again; then he stepped to one side and motioned to them to enter.

The woman was dressed in traditional clothes, cleverly fashioned so that they hinted at a svelte figure instead of completely concealing it. 'I am Mrs Ali; you want speak with my husband?' She had a voice that was slightly sing-song.

'If it's not too inconvenient,' replied Nick.

'You come.'

They followed her across the hall and into a very large, south-facing drawing-room which was furnished with such luxurious profligacy that the effect was one of ostentation rather than tactful elegance.

'Please, your name? I tell my husband.'

'I'm Nick Wood and this is my cousin, Judy Bowman. Judy has an uncle who met Mr Ali last year and when he heard she was coming up here, he asked her to call in and give Mr Ali his regards.' When they'd talked it over and decided what reason to give for their call, they'd reckoned that that was as good a reason as any, since it was casual and imprecise, but perfectly feasible; if Ali denied all memory of Judy's uncle, no suspicion would be aroused. But now, Nick suddenly had the sinking feeling that the falsity of what he'd said was terribly apparent.

Mrs Ali showed neither surprise nor suspicion. 'Karim like much to meet, but he is ill last week with . . .' She searched for the word, found it, ' . . . influenza.'

'I'm very sorry to hear that,' said Judy.

'Is sorry for everyone.' She smiled. 'Karim not like being ill and is very annoyed. Doctor say must drink a tonic, but no, he will not.' She shrugged her shoulders, an eloquent gesture which said that no wife could be responsible for her husband's follies. 'I go. If well, he is seeing you.' She asked Judy: 'Please, the name of uncle?'

'Miles Bowman. He worked in the Arabian Gulf for several years and apparently he and Mr Ali met last year and found they'd a lot in common. One of the things, I seem to remember, was scuba diving.' The little details, Judy had said earlier to Nick, were what made a lie believable. She had spoken with considerable authority.

'I speak. Please to sit.' She left the room, all her movements possessed of a natural elegance.

Waiting until certain it was safe to speak, Nick said, in a low voice: 'What d'you think?' Judy didn't answer, but shook her head. He couldn't make out whether this meant she had not yet formulated an opinion. As far as he was concerned, Mrs Ali's behaviour had been so natural and friendly that it was beginning to seem ridiculous to believe she could be hiding anything.

Judy indicated a richly inlaid pie-crust table to the right of the open fireplace with its elaborate overmantel. 'See that?'

'What about it?'

'The photographs, you gloop. See if any of them are of him.'

Instinctively, he looked at the nearer of the two doorways.

'She can't possibly come back yet. In any case, what's suspicious about having a look at some photos?'

The trouble was, he thought, knowing he was engaged in a deception, he had a guilty conscience. And a guilty conscience, as someone had once remarked, made one feel and act guilty . . . For once, he decided, he'd overcome such weakness. He'd act as if he'd every right in the world to do what he was doing . . .

'You know what?' She giggled. 'You look just like the villain in that golden oldie they showed last week.'

He ignored her. He studied the four photgraphs, each in a very heavy, over-ornamented silver frame. Three of them featured Mrs Ali and a heavily-bearded man, but they had been taken at too great a distance for details to be sharp;

superficially, the man resembled the one he had seen in the car, but it was impossible to say more than that. He told Judy so, then went over to one of the chairs and sat. Very soon afterwards they heard approaching footsteps and Judy, less at ease than her previous words might have suggested, quickly began a conversation about what they'd do that evening.

Mrs Ali entered the room. 'Very sorry, but Karim says he has very bad headache and is weak. He asks if all right he is not coming. But wishes much to meet you and talk on your uncle. Please to come to lunch on Monday when he is being much better.'

'There's really no need to go to all that trouble,' said Nick.

'Is no trouble. Karim much like talking with young people.'

'In that case, we'd love to come,' said Judy. 'Would it be best if we ring over the weekend to make certain that he is all right?'

'No need. He is being much better on Monday.'

'Then what time would you like us to arrive?'

'Please, about half-past twelve.'

'We'll be here.' Judy stood and Nick followed suit. 'Thanks so much for bothering to see us. We really are looking forward to Monday. And we do hope that Mr Ali will soon be well again.'

They left and said goodbye at the front door. They went out, mounted their bikes and rode off, after a last wave to Mrs Ali who remained standing in the porch. When they were halfway towards the brow of the rise, Nick said: 'That's answered that, then.'

'What's answered what?'

'She couldn't have been more at ease and less worried about anything. It can't have been her husband in the car.'

'So you're quite happy to accept that you've got a gloopy memory?'

'It's not like that . . .'

'So just what would you call a memory which tells its owner that a whole sequence of events took place when none of them did? Brilliant?'

'I can't help what a smack on the head did for me.'

'Are you referring to the one last week, or the one you obviously received when you were young?'

'Why are you suddenly so darned vinegary again?'

'Because you're being so wet that you'd dissolve into a sheet of blotting-paper . . . Can't you begin to appreciate that everything she did and said was designed to make you think and talk as you are now?'

'If anything funny were going on, d'you think she'd have invited us back on Monday to lunch?'

'Then you don't find that hightly significant?'

'Yes, I do. It means our suspicions are wrong.'

'I'll tell you what it means. She was doing everything she could think of to allay our suspicions.'

'Come off it, Judy. That's thinking twisted.'

'Thinking straight, unlike you who'd obviously believe in fairies at the bottom of the garden if she told you they were there . . . Just ask yourself one question. Why should she bother to invite us to lunch when she's never clapped eyes on us before and her husband couldn't remember Uncle Miles because there's no such person?'

'But she told you why. He likes talking to young people.'

They reached the brow of the hill and began to coast down towards the gates.

'Why Monday?' said Judy suddenly.

'Why not?'

'That's five days from now . . . This means that five days must represent some sort of critical period. And almost certainly it won't matter if the truth does come out on Monday.'

'The critical period just means he'll be over his flu.'

'Funny thing about his flu.'

'With you in the mood you're in right now, you'd find something funny about an obituary notice.'

'That all depends on whose.'

They passed the gatehouse, went through the gateway, slowed to make certain the road was clear, and then turned right on to it.

Nick said: 'There was a good place just this side of the fir trees.'

'What are you on about? A good place for what?'

'Lunch, of course.'

'Obviously both you and Napoleon's army shout *Vivre l'Intérieur*.'

'Highly amusing!'

Her tone became thoughtful. 'It's obvious the police spoke to Karim Ali – did they say anything about the interview to you?'

'Not much. Just that it was impossible he could be the man in the car because they'd seen his face and questioned him thoroughly.'

'You're sure the word "thoroughly" was used?'

'I don't know about the exact word. But it was certainly to that effect.'

'When was this interview?'

'Mr Johns told me about it on Saturday.'

'So probably it took place on Friday . . . According to Mrs Ali, her husband was ill last week and it's still hitting him. That means it's been a severe case. So they couldn't have questioned him thoroughly on Friday . . . Or if they did, he couldn't have had a severe case.'

'Why not?'

'If you'd ever suffered one, you wouldn't ask such a stupid question . . . The story she gave us was pure invention, to explain why he didn't meet us. And he didn't dare because he guessed who you were and why you'd called and he was afraid you'd identify him as an impostor.'

'And you've told me that I've too much imagination!'

They reached the place Nick had previously mentally marked down as a good picnic site and he called on Judy to stop. Grudgingly, she admitted that it was quite a pleasant spot. Grass sloped down to a small, quick-flowing brook and, since the land faced south, it gained the maximum amount of sunlight while being protected from the light wind.

Judy's humour quickly improved and as she spread out the

food, she said: 'Mary asked me if you had a good appetite. I told her a horse would be left at the starting-gate. She seems to have taken me literally. We'll never get through all this.'

He grinned. 'We can try.'

She poured out two mugfuls of Coke, then quartered a pork pie. She drank, ate a piece of pie. 'You know what we've got to do, don't you? Find some way you can have a really good look at the Karim Ali who's living in the house now.'

'No fuss. I'll be doing that on Monday.'

'After explaining everything to you in words of one syllable, you still haven't understood? They've no intention of giving us lunch on Monday. All that was just to keep us quiet.' She ate another piece of pie. 'I've an idea. If you asked your aunt if you could spend a night at Mary's, would she object?'

'I'm sure she wouldn't.'

'And I'm certain that if I told Mary we'd met some friends today who'd asked us to supper tomorrow evening and would it be all right if we stayed until the last train back, she'd OK that.'

'Where's all this leading to?'

'You really can be incredibly dense. We're going to return to Manners Deep tomorrow evening once it's dark and we'll scout around until you manage to get a really good look at Karim Ali. That way we'll know the truth, once and for all.'

Chapter 10

There was a scream to their right and Nick came to an abrupt halt, his stomach suddenly feeling as if it had been caught in a grip of ice. Then the sound was repeated and he belatedly identified it as the cry of a vixen. How, he asked himself as he moved forward once more, could he have been so stupid as to have agreed to her wild scheme? If only he'd had the sense to refuse to have anything to do with it, right now he'd be sitting in front of the television, watching the new comedy series which was supposed to be so funny . . .

'Is it much further?' she whispered.

'Can't you see the lights?'

'Yes, but . . .'

She was really nervous! It was a discovery which, in a strange way, bolstered his own somewhat shaky confidence.

There was a rustle of leaves from their right. She gave a muted cry and jumped forward to grip his arm.

'It's only a couple of pigeons flying off,' he said.

'Oh!' After a moment, she let go of his arm.

He led the way forward once more. There was plenty of cloud but it was not heavy and with a nearly full moon there was just enough light to be able to walk across the parkland without too much difficulty.

The house lights drew nearer and the bulk of the house became obvious against the sky. Judy had, when she'd planned the expedition, airily said that they'd find some way of getting a good look at the man who claimed to be Karim Ali, but even she had not been prepared to be specific about exactly how. Now, they would have to become specific.

'Some of the downstairs windows aren't curtained,' she whispered.

He'd come to the same conclusion slightly earlier. Uncurtained windows should make their task much easier . . . He wondered if there were any significance in the fact that so many of the rooms had lights on in them? If no one was in a room at home, all the lights in it were switched off to economise on electricity. But perhaps if one was really wealthy, one didn't bother about such mundane matters . . .

They reached a long hedge. He tried to recall from memory the house and grounds as he'd seen them the day before. To the south all the hedges had stopped well short of the house, but to the west, which was the direction from which they were now approaching, at least two of them had run almost up to it. So this one might offer both cover and direction. 'Keep close to the hedge,' he whispered.

'All right.'

From the moment they'd set foot inside the park, she'd become a different person. Gone was the Judy of forceful opinions and instead there was a Judy who was content to follow his lead without argument. A very great improvement!

They moved down the hedge, trying to avoid stepping on to any loose twigs. They had almost reached the house when they came to a gate. It was made of tubular metal and had been strung with wire-netting to prevent animals getting through. The catch was a simple bar. He started to swing the gate open, but stopped when it squeaked with a sound which, to his straining ears, had sounded loud enough to alert everyone in the house. But nothing happened and he realised that it had only seemed so loud because he was under such tension; to anyone only a few metres away it would have been barely audible and easily lost amongst all the other night sounds. More confidently, but more slowly, he opened it wide.

They passed through the gateway. Beyond was a grass path and then well-dug earth in which peas, staked out, were growing. The kitchen garden. He pointed at the grass to remind her to make certain she walked on that and did not step off on to the earth. He'd read only recently that a footprint could tell the police quite a lot about the person who'd made it.

69

They reached a second gate, this time made of wrought-iron. It swung open noiselessly, suggesting it had recently been oiled.

Light from the nearest window stretched out to illuminate a gravel path, half a rose-bed, and a small section of beautifully trimmed lawn. Keeping on the lawn, he went forward until just outside the edge of the shaft of light. From here, a small segment of the room was visible; there was a grand piano – of which he could see a third – and a small, ornate table with cabriole legs on which was a bowl of flowers. The music room, presumably. He turned. 'We need to move on,' he whispered. 'The best thing is to crawl.'

She briefly touched his arm to show she'd understood.

From the bottom of the window to the ground was something over a metre so there was a triangle of darkness, but almost all of this lay on the gravel path. Very, very slowly, he crawled along the gravel, managing to make far less noise than he had imagined he must. As soon as possible, he returned to the lawn. He stood. The next shaft of light was some five metres away and as they approached this they heard the sound of voices. Nick's sense of excitement sharpened. There were people in the room and the curtains weren't drawn. If Karim Ali was not lying in bed, suffering the debilitating effects of flu, but was in there, and if he bore only a superficial resemblance to the injured man in the Rover . . .

Part of the room came into view. He saw a sideboard on which stood two cut-glass decanters and a glass bowl of fruit, several glasses, and small pile of plates. They'd had the luck to arrive at dinner-time.

He moved forward until the edge of the shaft of light was almost brushing him. He still could not see anyone in the room. He pointed to show he was going to crawl once more and then led the way under the light. When he stood, he was between two shafts of light, the one ahead coming from the second window of the dining-room. He looked back, expecting to see further towards the centre of the room, but instead found himself staring at the corner. Only then did he realise that, given the angles involved, this was inevitable. Not until he was on the far side of the other window would he be able, hopefully, to see the centre of the room.

They walked forward, crawled under the light, stood. He saw a long table at which sat Mrs Ali and a man. The man had very black hair, slightly curly, a generous forehead, high cheekbones, a beaky nose, thick lips, and a full, very black, beard and moustache. As far as he could judge, the man in the Rover. But this man's cheek was patently unmarked. He turned to whisper to Judy, but at that second a torch was switched on and both of them were caught in the powerful beam.

Chapter 11

Instinct made Nick shout 'Run.' He whipped round to his right and took the first pace forward. Fingers, with a grip of steel, caught hold of his arm and then, using his own developing momentum, twisted him round and sent him crashing to the ground. He was momentarily winded.

'Nick!' Judy cried, her voice shrill. She knelt by his side. 'Are you hurt badly?'

He shook his head as he struggled to his knees, trying to draw in enough air to bring relief to his aching lungs. Hands hooked under his arm-pits and lifted him to his feet with little effort, despite his solid build.

He tried to take stock of the situation. Judy was by his side, her face expressing sharp worry and fear. Apart from whoever held the torch, he thought he could make out two men. So there was little chance of breaking free . . .

'Please into house,' said one of the men.

'We'd better go,' he said quietly. Judy reached out and gripped his hand, seeking all the support he could give her. A push in the back started him walking.

They went round the corner of the house to a side door. The man with the torch opened this and then stood to one side. 'Please,' he said, motioning to them to enter.

Too polite by far, thought Nick bitterly.

They were in a largish passage, along which were four doors, three on one side and one on the other, and between the doors hung a series of sporting prints. The nearest of these depicted a fox just before the hounds caught up with it. His sympathies were all with the fox.

'Please, here.'

The second door on the left was opened and they went

through to a room which, although furnished, had an air about it which suggested it was seldom used.

'There.' The man with the torch pointed at the doorway on the far side of the room.

Nick, as casually as possible, checked where the other two men were. One stood immediately behind Judy, the other had remained near the doorway they'd just come through. Neither Judy nor he would get more than a couple of paces . . .

'Please, in now.'

They went through to find themselves in the dining-room.

Karim Ali, at the far end of the table, stood, his movements slightly clumsy because of the plaster on his right leg. 'Good evening. Very nice to meet you both.'

Nick's thoughts did a heavy side-spin. He'd been braving himself for, at the very least, an angry scene, yet the manner of the meeting had suggested they were welcome guests.

'Please do not remain standing. Come and sit down at the table. You might like to join us at our meal if you have not eaten?'

Nick looked quickly at Judy, but she was obviously as bewildered as he.

'Don't feel you'll be depriving us. As always, the cook has prepared far more food than we could possibly want for two meals, let alone one.'

'You eat,' said Mrs Ali, with a smile.

Feeling as if this were a time of dream-logic, Nick approached the table. Karim Ali leaned over, while holding on to the table with one hand, to pull out the chair on his right. 'Nick, I suggest you sit here. And Miss Bowman – or may I say Judy? – perhaps you will sit on the other side, next to my wife?' He turned and spoke briefly to the three men in Arabic; they left.

Judy and Nick sat; Karim Ali did the same. He said, his voice lightly amused: 'I expect you wonder how it is that yesterday I was so ill I could not come downstairs to see you and talk about Judy's uncle – and I'm very sorry, but I have to confess I do not remember meeting him, but we'll talk

73

about that later – whilst today I am here, eating an excellent meal? I, myself, am surprised how quickly I recovered; and am duly grateful.'

'No surprise,' said Mrs Ali. 'Yesterday, not truly ill.'

He smiled briefly. 'My wife always believes that men make a fuss over nothing, merely to gain sympathy. Perhaps she is correct sometimes, but I assure you that yesterday she was very wrong . . . Now, Judy, help yourself to whatever you would like. I am sorry it is only a cold meal but when we are not expecting guests, and are on our own, we eat simply.'

She pulled her thoughts together. Simple was a word open to different definitions. A choice of beef, lamb, chicken, quail, and meat loaf, two kinds of potato mayonnaise, cole-slaw, lettuce salad, baby beets and pickled gherkins would not be simple according to many people . . .

Karim Ali asked: 'What would you like to drink? Orange-ade, lemonade, or Coke?'

'Coke, please,' replied Judy.

Nick saw neither of them make any movement, yet the door at the opposite end of the room opened and a woman, noticeably dark-skinned, stepped just inside. Mrs Ali spoke in Arabic. The woman left, closing the door behind her. One of them obviously had a call-button, operated by foot. So the alarm could be given the second either Judy or he made the first move to escape . . . But escape from what? A dinner party to which they had not been invited, but at which they were welcome guests?

'You look perhaps a little . . . how shall we say? Bothered?' said Karim Ali.

Nick jerked his mind back to the immediate present. 'I'm sorry. It's just . . .' He came to a stop.

'It is, perhaps, that you are wondering whether I am the true Karim Ali, owner of this house?'

Nick's sense of embarrassment was acute and he could feel his cheeks reddening.

The maid returned to the dining-room and served Judy and Nick with Coca-Cola, then left. Karim Ali asked Nick to help

74

himself to meat, which he did, grateful for something to do since this helped to ease his embarrassment.

Karim Ali wiped his mouth on a beautifully embroidered serviette, then said: 'Let me assure you, there is absolutely no cause to be upset. The question why you came here interests me, it does not anger me in the least.'

Yet again, Nick looked briefly at Karim Ali's right cheek. The skin was smooth and unblemished and it was ridiculous to imagine he could recently have been in that car crash. But was he the man in the car? (Or, to put it more logically, was he the man Nick imagined he'd seen in the car?) Nick found it increasingly difficult to picture the face in the car; inevitably, the remembered image became fused into the one in front of him so that any differences – if there were any; he now couldn't place any – were lost . . .

Karim Ali spoke with a sudden earnestness. 'Nick, as I believe you must know, there has been a very serious mistake which resulted in the police accusing me of dealing in drugs. It is a terrible, painful lie. I would never do such a thing because I know how vicious is the drug trade; not a king's ransom would make me do such a thing and soon I will prove this . . . But because of these troubles, the police came to find out whether my face is injured.' He ran the fingers of his right hand across his cheek. 'They discovered it wasn't. And my car has not had an accident.

'So now I am very interested. How could you imagine you saw me, injured, in the back of my car? I will tell you. There is only one feasible explanation. ESR. Do you understand that?'

Nick shook his head.

'You'll have heard of ESP – extra-sensory perception. For many years, people have been arguing as to whether there is such a thing. But there is no argument about ESR – extra-sensory retrieval. Time and time again – ever since people have no longer been scared of being labelled mental if they admit to having experienced it – this has been shown to be fact; even to the doubting Thomases who would doubt their own evidence if that were not to negate those very doubts. Put simply, the term just means the ability of the human mind occasionally to retrieve a perfectly clear memory which is based on facts yet is in itself completely false. The interesting and important question regarding ESR is why? . . . The mind endlessly surprises and fascinates. We don't even know where it is situated, yet it is responsible for all human achievement. Its powers have no definite limits and probably we are using only a fraction of such powers because of ignorance or prejudice. Yet, paradoxically, that ignorance and those prejudices owe their existence to it. Could any subject be more fascinating? This is why, when I heard of the ESR you had experienced, I determined to learn all I could about it because then perhaps I might be allowed to lift one corner of the veil which covers 'why?'. And when my wife told me you had actually called here . . . Personally, I think it is why my health improved so rapidly! So now I hope you will understand why I am going to ask you many, many questions.'

'You ask nothing until Nick eat,' said Mrs Ali.

'But . . .'

'He has hunger.'

He shrugged his shoulders, his expression wry. 'Obviously, I'm going to have to contain my impatience. But when the meal is finished, then I will ask – have you, Nick, ever met me before; have you seen photographs of me; did the man in the car truly resemble me?'

Nick guessed from Judy's expression that her thoughts paralleled his. Karim Ali's manner was so straightforward and friendly, his interest in events so untroubled, it was clearly ridiculous to suspect him any longer of being an imposter. Despite their seeming clarity, those memories of the crashed car and injured passenger which Nick had were false, and he had not been coshed, he had been struck by a falling branch of an oak tree. His mind had flipped . . . but only temporarily! ESR. Extra-sensory retrieval. Something that throughout the ages had occurred to people and frightened them, but now was the subject of careful investigation. He began to be proud of his experience, rather than ashamed . . .

Judy looked across the drawing-room at the beautifully inlaid grandmother clock with the painted face. 'We really must leave if we're to catch our train.'

'I'm sorry you have to go so soon,' said Karim Ali. 'It has been a very interesting evening . . . One thing before you leave, please do come to lunch on Monday; I would like to see more of you.' He chuckled. 'And honesty compels me to admit that by then I will have other questions to ask!'

Judy stood. 'We'll look forward to that. And thank you so much for dinner.'

'It has been our pleasure.'

They left the drawing-room and went into the hall.

'You have coats?' asked Karim Ali. 'It sounds as if the wind is blowing more strongly and you may find it has become rather cold.'

'They're with our bikes,' replied Nick.

'And where are they?'

'Er . . . Under a hedge by the road,' he admitted shame-facedly.

Karim Ali laughed. And, because he held his head back, a gold-capped tooth gleamed with reflected light.

Nick's mind flicked back to the memory he held of that car crash – a memory that only three-quarters of an hour ago he had finally decided must be false because Karim Ali's face was unmarked and his manner so open and easy. He was sure that the man in the car had had false teeth. This man's teeth were obviously his own. Then here was a difference which, while in one sense small, was so specific it must surely rest on fact, not on a memory twisted by ESR? Then were there, after all, two men, one impersonating the other, had there been a crashed car, had he been coshed and moved and, despite all the contradictory evidence, should he have believed in and trusted his memory throughout?

His surprise and uncertainty were obvious. Unwittingly, Karim Ali answered Nick's questions as his expression changed to one of anger.

Chapter 12

There was a long silence, which Karim Ali broke; his voice was hard. 'I shall be very interested to discover what you have just learned.'

Judy, unable to judge what had happened, but warned by Karim Ali's attitude, moved closer to Nick in an instinctive appeal for protection.

Nick judged that their only chance now was to break free immediately, before any help could be summoned. 'Come on,' he shouted, banking on surprise to gain them a few vital seconds. He raced across to the front door and struggled to open this.

'It's locked electrically,' said Karim Ali.

Nick whirled round. He saw two men entering the hall through one of the far doorways. The wide staircase, which split into two at a half-landing, lay equidistant from Judy and himself and the two men. If they could make that ... A heavy blow to the side of the head sent him staggering sideways.

'Don't be so stupid,' said Karim Ali contemptuously. He waited until Nick was once more standing upright. 'Now. What told you the truth?'

There seemed to be no point in refusing to answer. 'I saw your gold tooth when you laughed. The man in the car had false ones.'

'How true is our saying, "Triumph walks, disaster creeps." It's very unfortunate for you that you are observant, otherwise you could have left here unharmed.' He fingered his beard as he studied them. 'At dinner, Nick, you said you were staying the night with Judy and her friends. Judy, did you tell your friends where you were coming this evening?'

'Yes, I did,' she answered bravely. 'And what's more, I explained why and said that if we weren't back on the last train they were to get in touch with the police.'

'You must consider me to be exceedingly gullible if you imagine I will believe that they would have allowed you to make the journey if they had had the slightest idea of what you truly intended doing. So what did you really say to them?'

'I've just told you.'

Karim Ali gave a signal and one of the men came forward, gripped Nick's left arm and wrenched it round and up behind his back in a grip that caused immediate and sharp pain.

'Stop it,' shouted Judy.

'Certainly. The moment you tell me the truth.'

'I said we were having supper with a school friend of mine.' Her voice was uneven.

'And where is this friend supposed to live?'

She hesitated, saw Karim Ali was about to give another signal, and said desperately: 'Elkeld.'

'Which lies, does it not, in the opposite direction to here?' He thought for a moment, nodded, and Nick's arm was released. He began to pace the floor, but almost immediately came to a stop because the plaster made his movements so clumsy; he bent down and removed the plaster, which proved to have been in two halves cleverly held together by concealed straps.

Nick said urgently: 'If you let us go, I promise I won't tell the police anything.'

'You expect me to accept a promise you can break with impunity as soon as you're away from here?'

'But I won't break it.'

He shrugged his shoulders. He spoke to the two men in Arabic, and then to Judy and Nick in English. 'For certain reasons, I have to make sure that for the next few days you cannot tell the police what you have learned; after that, it will not matter. So you must stay in this house. But this naturally raises a problem. If you do not return to where you are meant to be staying, the alarm will be given. That might just bring

79

the police here. So I have to make certain that everyone believes you to be safe and staying with someone else . . . Judy, in a moment, you will telephone your friends in Keir Brook and you will tell them that you and Nick have been asked to stay at Elkeld. Nick, tomorrow you will telephone your friends in Stillthwaite and you will tell them that you've been asked to stay with Judy for another day or two.' He paused. 'A word of warning. I shall be listening on an extension and if either of you tries to raise an alarm, the other will suffer immediately.

'One final thing. Do not be silly and spend your time thinking of escape. Escape is impossible and can only lead to suffering if you attempt it. Whilst if you do exactly as you are told, soon you will be free to leave, quite unharmed. Do you understand?'

Judy looked at Nick; Nick muttered an answer.

'Good. Then now you, Nick, will go upstairs.'

Nick stared at Judy, reluctant to leave her on her own. A sharp prod in the back sent him stumbling forward. As he regained his balance, he realised with sickening certainty that for the moment there was really nothing they could do. He started walking towards the staircase, his mind filled with the image of Judy, frightened and appealing to him for the help he could not give.

Chapter 13

The room he was locked up in was small and in a poor state of decoration – almost certainly, he thought, it had been a servant's bedroom in the old days. There was practically no furniture – just a bed, with only a mattress on it, a kitchen chair, and a chest-of-drawers which had seen many better days.

He went over to the small sash window and carefully lifted the lower half. Below was the large courtyard, well illuminated by several lights. He visually examined the wall of the house and immediately came to the conclusion that there was no way of climbing down it – no stout, ancient creeper, no convenient drain-pipe. He looked up. The guttering was out of reach and it was impossible to gain any idea of what the roof was like.

He crossed to the door. It was old, but stout; to break it down would call for considerable effort and, inevitably, noise. Karim Ali had made a point of the fact that each of them was a hostage for the other, so a botched attempt to escape could only mean that Judy would be hurt . . .

The corridor was uncarpeted and he heard the approach of footsteps. These came to a stop, the lock clicked, and the door opened. The man who'd brought him up fifteen minutes earlier came in and threw a pillow and a sheet on to the mattress. 'Blanket after,' he said before he left, locking the door behind him.

Nick's mind raced. If the man came on his own next time, how to overpower him . . . It was clearly a stupid question. Nick was strong, but it was the strength of his age, not of maturity; he wouldn't stand a chance in a straight fight. So the only result of any such action would be disaster . . .

He sat down on the edge of the bed and there was a quick

squeak of metal from the ancient, crude springs which were in the form of a diamond-shaped lattice. Karim Ali had told them that if they didn't cause any trouble, in a few days' time they'd be allowed to go free. Wasn't the sensible thing to do to forget all about escape?

Once again, there was the sound of footsteps. Two people this time, he judged. Judy and her guard? The sounds passed his door, grew fainter, then stopped. A little later, he heard a door being shut. If Judy had been one of the two, she had been put into a room close to, or at, the end of the corridor.

The footsteps grew louder as one person returned. It might help tremendously to know that the second person had been Judy because then he would have fixed the position of her prison . . . He stood. 'Hey,' he shouted. 'Hey, I want something.'

The lock clicked, the door was opened by the man who had remained in the hall with Judy. 'You want?' His expression was sullen, not wary.

'I wonder if you could find me some books to read? Otherwise, there's nothing to do.'

'No.'

'Surely you could find something? I mean, the library must be full of books . . .'

'You not need.' The man stepped back, pulled the door shut, and locked it.

The odds were, Nick thought, that the second person *had* been Judy . . . His elation at having hit back at his captors by discovering something which might prove important didn't last long. If it was too dangerous to try to escape, what did it really signify that now he could be reasonably certain he knew where she was being held? He sat on the bed again; it squeaked more teeth-twitchingly than before.

Karim Ali had said that in a few days' time Judy and he would be free to go. That must mean that something was happening within the next few days that was vital to their plans. (He remembered Judy's comments on the invitation to lunch on Monday.) What could that something be? . . .

Karim Ali had refused to accept their word that if set free they'd not tell the police what had happened. So he must be assuming that when he did release them, they'd immediately get on to the police. Was he intending to disappear the moment he released them? Nick's thoughts became grim. Karim Ali had spoken blithely about keeping their disappearance hidden by working it so that everyone who was interested in their whereabouts would believe them safe and sound with someone else. But how long could he believe that such a deception would last? Ten to one, when Aunt Caroline was telephoned tomorrow, she would, at the very least, want his telephone number so that she could keep in touch with him; and it was more than possible that, in fact, she would not be at all happy for him to stay away another night since she was primarily responsible for him and he was her guest. So she might agree to one night only with reluctance and would refuse any longer stay . . .

The bogus Karim Ali had proved himself a consummate liar. In a very short space of time, he'd hoodwinked both Judy and himself into believing that he was the genuine Karim Ali and that Nick's memory of the crash *was* faulty, the result of ESR. So what more likely than that he was lying about his future intentions?

The man who'd refused a moment ago to bring him any books had said, 'You not need.' Then, it had seemed that he'd meant that since the books weren't essential, he couldn't be bothered to find any. But what if he'd meant those words literally, in the sense that soon Nick wouldn't be around to read?

Assume that Karim Ali appreciated how difficult it must prove to be to conceal their disappearance for the next few days, that when he did release them they'd report what had happened to the police who would immediately start searching for him . . . Wouldn't the simplest solution from his point of view be to arrange an 'accident' somewhere *en route* from Elkeld? A hit and run car which had knocked into two cyclists who were returning home in

83

the dark, having missed the last train?

He tried to fault such a conclusion, because it was so brutally unacceptable. But even as he did so, part of his mind reminded him that it had been reached logically and to turn away from it would be to blind himself because he did not have the courage to see.

He stood, crossed to the window, and again looked down at the courtyard. Accept everything and then Judy and he just had to escape. But he had previously come to another logical conclusion – to try to escape could only lead to disaster . . . If only he could have talked it over with her. She'd have seen more clearly all the dangers, the probabilities, the possibilities. But she was locked up in a room along the corridor and there was no way of talking to her.

He leaned out of the window. He'd accepted that there was no way of escape here, but then he had believed that escape was an option; now, he was convinced it was a necessity. So what had previously offered nothing might now be seen to offer something . . . A direct drop to the concrete was out of the question; such a fall must end in broken bones. The windows on either side were at least three metres away, with nothing to help bridge the gap. The pointing of the brickwork was in good order, leaving no gaps between bricks which might just have offered toe- and finger-holds to someone desperate. The guttering remained out of reach . . . There was no way of escape through the window. And even if there had been, he daren't go on his own and leave Judy behind.

He turned, crossed to the door, and examined it far more thoroughly than before. It was old, but solid; the lock looked strong; the hinges were hidden.

He returned to the bed and slumped down on it, with a repeat of the accompaniment of squeaks. What did one do when one had to do something, but there was nothing one could do? When the real Karim Ali had been in the car crash, it had been necessary to prove that he was uninjured and the car undamaged. Impossible. Yet they'd almost managed to do the impossible by bluff. Couldn't he now take a leaf out of their book and use bluff to escape?

There was no way of escape via the window, so it had to be via the door. Since there was no possibility of breaking down the door or forcing the lock, escape was only possible when the door had been opened from the outside. Before very long it would be opened by someone bringing blankets. Impossible to overcome him silently – or noisily, for that matter – by direct physical action. How to get the better of him by bluff . . . He'd almost given up, when an idea began to form.

He had to assume that there was little time left. He stood, went over to the chair, and examined it. Meant for constant and rough use, it had been built strongly and the legs were thick, but where they fitted into the underneath of the seat two of them were worm-eaten. He put the chair on the ground and applied increasing pressure on one of the worm-eaten legs. The wood creaked, but did not crack. He needed to exert far more pressure if he were to break off that leg. A really sharp blow might do it, but that would create noise and if someone came to find out what was happening, that would be that. So how to cut out the noise?

He stripped the pillowcase off the pillow, carefully wound it round the end of one of the worm-eaten legs. He raised the chair up, brought it down on the mattress. There was little sound, but equally the blow had considerably less effect than it would have done if delivered against a hard surface. The leg was as firmly fixed as before. He slammed the chair down a second time, a third, a fourth . . . There was a splintering of wood and the leg broke off at the base, while still attached to the side rails. Sweating, as much from excitement as exertion, he wrenched the leg free. He gripped the un-worm-eaten end in both hands. A fairly formidable weapon.

He dumped the rest of the chair over against the wall, on the hinge side of the door, leant the leg against the wall, ready to be grabbed in a hurry. He returned to the bed, picked up the sheet and tried to tear it in half. But even though he used all his strength, so that his hands began to shake, he could not tear the folded edge. It was not a problem he had foreseen and for a moment it defeated him. Was there anything in the room with a sharp edge? . . . The bed squeaked whenever he sat on it, which suggested it was old and crudely made. One of the wire hooks which held the diamond-shaped lattice against the solid frame might, then, have an edge that could be used as a blade. He pushed the mattress off the bed. Some of the hooks did have crude, sharp ends. He chose the one which was widest. Holding the sheet in both hands, he worked the edge against the end of the hook. For a time it seemed he was getting nowhere, then suddenly he was through. After that, it was easy to rip the sheet down its centre; when the tear reached the bottom edge, he cut through that. He tore the sheet twice more and this gave him four strips. These he tied to each other. Now he had something to use as a rope.

Slowly, carefully, he moved the bed across the floor until close to the window, when he swung one end round so that it abutted the wall. He tied one end of his rope to a leg of the bed, coiled the rest on the window-sill, not daring to push it out until the very last moment in case it was seen from below.

Now it was a case of waiting. Words vaguely remembered drifted through his mind. Something about waiting and not getting tired of waiting . . . Judy would very quickly have provided the full and correct quote. In any case, it ought to read 'not get scared by waiting'. Waiting let the mind roam, so that it dwelt on all the things which could go wrong, with disastrous consequences . . .

There was the sound of footsteps coming closer. He pushed the coil of sheeting out of the window, made certain its course from the bed leg over the window-sill was obvious, ran across to the inside wall. He picked up the chair leg.

The footsteps passed the door. The sudden loss of tension made him feel sick. Maybe he wasn't to be given a blanket. After all, if he'd no need for a book to read, by the same token he'd no need for a blanket to keep him warm. Perhaps that had been said merely to fool him into believing he had a future . . .

The footsteps returned. They came to a stop. He raised the

chair leg. The lock made its familiar snick of sound and he tightened his already tight two-handed grip. The door swung open.

The man took one pace forward, came to a sharp stop. He saw the bed had been moved to act as an anchor-weight, the window was open, and a rope made from sheeting had been thrown out of the window. Instinctively, he accepted the natural explanation for what he saw and he ran forward to look out of the window to check if Nick was still in sight.

Nick raced forward on his stockinged feet and brought the chair leg down with all the strength he could muster. It broke in two and the far end spun off and hit the wall. The man staggered sideways, tried to reach out for support, collapsed to the ground and lay still.

Nick hauled in the sheeting, intending to untie it and to use the pieces as a gag and bonds, but there was a shout from downstairs. Seconds later, this was repeated and now it was possible to catch the sense of rapidly growing concern in the caller's voice. Something, perhaps the noise the piece of chair leg had made when it hit the wall, perhaps the thump of the man as he'd collapsed, had caught the caller's attention. When there was no reply, he'd hurry upstairs to find out what was wrong. So there was now not the time to gag and bind the man on the floor, already showing signs of regaining consciousness.

He picked up his shoes, raced out of the room and down the corridor, his feet making little noise on the bare floorboards. The penultimate door was unlocked and slightly ajar; the last one was locked, with the key in place. He unlocked it.

Judy had been making the bed, using the two blankets which she had just been given. When the door crashed open, her first reaction was apprehension, followed by defiance; when she realised the newcomer was Nick, surprised relief swamped all other emotions.

'Come on, move,' he said urgently.

She dropped the corner of the bedclothes she had been about to tuck in under the mattress, raced over to the door.

'We've got to . . .' He stopped abruptly as he heard the sounds of someone climbing the upper flight of stairs which, like the corridor, were uncarpeted. This corridor was a dead-end, so their only way of escape was either down, or past, the stairs; now, they were cut off from them . . . They had only one chance left. He grabbed her hand and pulled her along to the next room, opened the door more fully and led the way inside. He motioned to her to settle behind the door, then pushed that back to the position in which it had been before. Another bluff, based on the hope that they'd never imagine that Judy and he would have the nerve to hide in a room with an open door.

They heard the oncomer enter the room in which Nick had been held. There were voices, one speaker mumbling. Then there was a shout of alarm.

The man ran past the opened door and into the next, end room. He returned and started back down the corridor, suddenly stopped. Nick experienced a tension so sharp that he found it difficult to breathe and beads of perspiration prickled his neck and back. Had he, in his desperate hurry, left something behind in the corridor which pin-pointed where they were now? Or had the man outside realised that in the time available to them, they simply could not have gone far . . .

The man continued back towards the stairs. Judy gave a small gasp of relief. Nick turned to face her, grinned, and held up a thumb. She tried to smile back, but couldn't because she knew as well as he that the next few minutes were going to be even more critical.

Chapter 14

They heard a new voice – that of Karim Ali. It became obvious that he was coming upstairs and the same thought occurred to each of them. He was resourceful and clever; would he now be clever enough to work out what must have happened?

Karim Ali went into the one bedroom, spoke briefly, left and came along the corridor. Judy reached out for Nick's hand and he gripped hers reassuringly.

Another man followed Karim Ali and the two of them went into the end bedroom. An order, sharp and concise, was given and the second man left and returned along the corridor. Karim Ali stood in the doorway, talking to himself in a hard, angry voice; then there was a call from downstairs and he shouted an answer, left, and hurried to the stairs.

Nick released Judy's hand, crossed to the window and looked down at the courtyard. A man came out of the house, went over to the coach-house and inside. An engine started up and then a Land Rover backed out. It turned and went through the gateway into the park, heading for the boundary wall, its headlights on full beam and dancing as the vehicle bucked and jolted to the undulations of the ground. It had just gone out of sight, cut off by the edge of the house, when a second man went into the garage and drove out a green Rover. He turned into the park in the opposite direction to that which the Land Rover had taken. It needed little imagination to realise that the two cars were going to circle the park to ensure that neither captive managed to break free.

With two men out in the park, there were at least two more and two women in the house. Obviously, thought Nick, their best chance of escaping the house was when there were the least number of people in it. How they were then to elude the patrolling vehicles was another question for which he had not, as yet, the answer.

He returned to Judy and briefly whispered what he'd seen. 'So we try and break out now. But first we'll pick up a couple of pieces of the chair I smashed – that'll give us something to use if we need it.'

She nodded, but it was as obvious to her as to him that such weapons were little more than morale boosters now their escape was known.

'Take your shoes off.'

She removed them.

'Leave 'em here.' Even though he was sure that they would be glad of them later, the disadvantages of carrying them were too great.

He opened the door more fully and listened. From somewhere below he could just hear a man shouting, otherwise all was quiet. He stepped into the corridor and motioned Judy to follow him.

They knew just a little about the layout of the house. The main staircase led only up to the first floor; access to the top floor was by another, very utilitarian, one, situated beyond a door that was lined with green baize. Briefly discussing the problem, they came to the conclusion that the house was still divided into two separate worlds, those of upstairs and downstairs. This surely must mean that there would be another staircase from the domestic quarters directly up to the servants' bedrooms, since the servants would not have been expected to pass through the main part of the house unless their duties took them that way. It seemed better to make for the domestic quarters since these would almost certainly consist of a large number of small rooms – apart from the kitchen – whilst they knew already that the reception rooms were large and therefore easily checked by searchers.

They went along the corridor and into the room in which he'd been imprisoned, where they chose two pieces of the broken chair, then continued to the head of the staircase which they'd earlier ascended. They could hear no one. He signalled and they moved across.

The corridor made a right-angled turn and this brought them to the second staircase. They started down this, moving carefully, ready to turn and bolt back if discovered. There was a small, stuffy landing on the first floor, with no communicating door, and a second flight of stairs, steeper than the first. This ended in an area about two metres square which had doors on opposite sides. He listened at each in turn and heard nothing. Left or right? He looked at her, but she shook her head. Their lives probably depended on their choosing correctly, but they had nothing on which to base their choice.

'Try left,' she finally said. 'It's four letters and four's one of my lucky numbers.'

However illogically based, it was a decision. He turned the handle of the left-hand door and pushed. The door refused to move. Then it was going to have to be the right-hand door . . .

He pulled the door and it opened, the hinges creaking momentarily. The room beyond had a flagstone floor, twin sinks made from stone, and tiled walls; some kind of wash-room. They entered.

There were two doors. He judged from the single window, too high up to look out of, that the one on the right led directly outside and he tried to open this, but it was locked and there was no key. He opened the left-hand door. There was a passage and then the kitchen, a blaze of light; halfway along the passage, on the right, was another door. As he reached the door a woman in the kitchen called out and he came to an abrupt stop, fearful he had been spotted. But then there was silence and nothing to suggest an alarm and it became obvious she'd no idea they were nearby.

The room on the right was a store-room; bottles and tins were stacked on the shelves. There was no window.

'We'll have to try to go through the kitchen,' Judy whispered. 'That's bound to have access to the outside.'

He looked down at the chair leg in his right hand. No

matter what, he could not hit a woman . . .

He went forward until, while still outside the square of direct light, he could see almost half the kitchen. It was modernised and luxuriously equipped. Mrs Ali stood by a working surface and she was writing. She stopped, looked up, and called out again. She listened to the answer, wrote briefly once more. Then she reached across to a wall-mounted telephone, lifted the receiver, dialled, paused, dialled again, this time for very much longer. She waited, tapping on the working surface with the fingers of her free hand.

After a while, she replaced the receiver. She called out yet again, was answered. She muttered something to herself, walked rapidly to her left and out of sight. A door was slammed shut.

It seemed she had gone out of the kitchen, but because he could see only part of it he could not be certain. And even if it was now empty, whilst the lights were on it might so easily prove to be a trap. Yet if they were to reach the outside . . . 'Let's go,' he said hoarsely.

He moved slowly until he could see the whole of the kitchen. It was empty. There were two other doors. One to the left, which was the way Mrs Ali had been heading when she'd gone out of sight, one to the right. Because of all the twists and turns they'd taken, it was difficult to be certain of directions, but as far as he could judge, outside lay to the right.

'Make for the door on the right,' he whispered. He ran forward and reached the door, only to realise that Judy was not immediately behind him. He looked round, afraid she must have fallen, but saw that she'd crossed over to the working surface above which was the telephone. He wanted to shout, to remind her that every split second mattered and their good luck couldn't hold indefinitely . . . It didn't. As she turned round and began to run over, a man, obviously expecting Mrs Ali still to be present since he began talking immediately, hurried into the kitchen through the left-hand doorway. When he saw Judy and Nick, he came to an abrupt halt.

Nick wrenched open the door. The man recovered his wits and began to shout an alarm. They'd lost, Nick thought. Yet even whilst he accepted that logically this must be true, he determinedly fought on.

Beyond the kitchen was yet another short passage, at the end of which was a door in the lock of which was a key. The door proved to give access to the courtyard. He waved Judy past him, pulled out the key, slammed the door shut and locked it just before their pursuer grabbed the handle.

'Where now?' she panted.

Where indeed? The Rover and Land Rover were circling the park, creating a barrier that it was virtually impossible to break through unseen. Yet every second they stayed where they were gave their pursuers more time to head them off . . .

'Over to the garage,' he shouted as he began to run.

There were four sets of doors, three of which were open. Inside were a Fiat and a Granada, the latter was opposite a set of open doors. He raced over to it, pulled open the driving door, and checked the keys were in the ignition lock. 'Get in.'

She ran round and settled in the front passenger seat. 'Have you ever driven before?' she asked breathlessly.

'No. So fix the safety-belt. But it's an automatic so there can't be anything much to it.' He switched on the engine; it fired immediately. He selected reverse, looked in the rear-view mirror and saw two men enter the garage. Forgetting any need for caution, he slammed the accelerator down as he released the handbrake, the pedal biting into his stockinged foot. The engine coughed once, indignant at being asked to do so much so suddenly, then screamed up to high revs as the leading man reached out to a door handle. The car shot backwards, sending the one man flying and the other frantically diving for safety.

As they came into the light of the courtyard, Nick desperately tried to control the car and he wrenched the wheel round; this sent them into a tight reverse circle which had the tyres screaming and pouring out rubber smoke. Braking as hard as he could, he eventually managed to bring the car to a rocking halt, activating their inertia seat-belts.

By pure chance, they ended up facing the gateway. A man ran towards them, a spring-loaded cosh in his hand. Nick put the selector to drive and, ignoring experience, again floored the accelerator. The tyres scrabbled for a split second, then they gained a grip; the car catapulted forward and the on-coming man had to throw himself to one side to prevent being run down.

They were heading directly for the right-hand pillar of the gateway. 'Turn the wheel,' Judy shouted.

He spun the wheel over, dazed by the frantic speed with which everything was happening. The car skidded slightly just before they struck the brick pillar a glancing blow that sent fragments of bricks flying. Then they were through.

They charged across the gravel path and hit the slightly raised grassland with a force that thumped the suspension. They bounded forward.

'Put the lights on,' she cried, remembering with an impend-ing sense of catastrophe all the trees which grew at irregular intervals.

'I don't know which switch it is.'

'Press the lot, you idiot.'

Typical! he thought, meaning her rudeness. He depressed every switch and button he could find. Fans started up, wind-screen wipers began their monotonous arcs, jets of water dis-torted vision until cleared by the wipers, hazard lights flashed; then finally the headlights came on in dipped position. Im-mediately ahead of them was an oak tree with a trunk some one and a half metres in diameter. She gave a quick cry and closed her eyes. He spun the wheel over. They bounced into and out of a rabbit hole, just missed the tree.

If they'd kept any sort of direction since leaving the court-yard, he thought – as soon as he was capable of thinking coherently – it had been northerly, leaving them heading away from the main gates. But a park of this size must have more than one set of gates, so that somewhere ahead of them there was probably another. He increased speed slightly, beginning to be caught up in the thrill of driving across the grass.

Headlights appeared, coming in from the right. The Land Rover, he judged, noting how the lights were set high and close together. Unless there was radio communication between the house and the vehicles, the driver would not know that Judy and he had broken out in the Granada . . . He fiddled with the levers on the steering-column and discovered how to engage main beams. He flicked the lights to dip, to main beam, to dip, and back to main beam. The Land Rover came to a stop as the driver accepted the flashing as a signal to do so. The Granada shot past it.

Now they could see the brick wall. To their left, it stretched into darkness; to their right there was a break, and leading up to this what seemed to be a narrow driveway.

They bounced their way forward, swerving violently to miss a pollard-ash, and reached the driveway, gravel-surfaced and not so narrow as it had first looked. This brought them to the gateway. A pair of gates, clumsy in design when compared with those at the main entrance, were shut, and in the headlights they could see that for extra security these were secured by chain and padlock. He braked to a halt, at a loss to know which way to go now.

'Nick,' she said urgently, 'the second car's in sight and the first one's turning this way.'

Even if they did not have radio contact, probably the way the Granada had been driven had told its own story. What chance did he have of out-driving them? None, he decided. It was only luck which had got them this far in one piece.

'You must move or they'll have us cornered.'

And once cornered, that would be that. They wouldn't hesitate to use whatever force proved necessary. He looked to his right and left. Judy had got one thing wrong, he thought grimly; they were virtually cornered already. But they hadn't given in before when it had seemed they were in a hopeless situation and weren't going to start doing so now. 'Hang on all you can.'

'What are you going to do?'

By way of an answer, he floored the accelerator yet again. The revs rose to a scream, the back wheels dug down into the soft earth before finding a grip which sent the car surging forward. He aimed for the middle of the gates, but as every bump and dip jerked at the wheel, he knew it was going to be a matter of chance . . .

They hit the gates. There was the harsh, ugly sound of metal smashing into metal; the right headlamp went out; something was flung against the windscreen but this, being laminated, did not shatter . . . The bearing pins tore free of the ancient mortar and the gates, still joined by chain and padlock, were flung forward. The car surged over them, bouncing violently.

Careless of their speed and the fact that the treads of their tyres were still filled with earth, Nick swung the wheel over to turn on to the road. The rear of the car began to slide. Desperately struggling to control events, he wrenched the wheel this way and that and somehow managed to put on opposite lock at the vital moment to kill the skid. They raced on.

'Nick,' Judy said in a shaky voice, 'have you forgotten that in this country we usually drive on the left?'

All he'd been worrying about had been staying on the road, never mind which side. But, of course, there were other road users . . . 'How close are the others?'

She looked back. 'There's no sign of them.'

He took his foot off the accelerator and steered for the left-hand side of the road. They hit the grass verge, but not very hard. There was, he decided, a little more to driving a car than he had imagined.

They entered a village and saw some way ahead a public call-box. After Judy had checked there was still no sign of pursuit, Nick braked to a halt. He went into the call-box, dialled 999, and reported events. The PC in the control room at county HQ overcame his initial suspicions that this was a hoax and said that a patrol car would be with them in under five minutes.

96

Nick returned to the Granada. 'They'll be here in less than five minutes.'

'You mean we needn't drive any further? Thank heavens for small mercies!'

'I was doing all right.'

'By whose standards?'

'Maybe it was a bit hairy at times – but I got us away.'

She turned to face him. 'Yes, you did, Nick.' She touched his arm in a gesture that said far more than her words. 'And I'm quite certain there aren't many others who'd have managed to do that.'

Chapter 15

Detective Inspector Basdon stood in the centre of the master bedroom in Manners Deep and looked around him. Drawers had been opened and their contents scattered anywhere, clothes had been pulled out of cupboards and left in ragged piles on the floor; a small safe, normally hidden behind a painting, was open and empty. They'd grabbed what was essential and fled . . .

Nick Woods had been right from the beginning. There *had* been a car accident in which Karim Ali *had* been injured whilst breaking one of the conditions of his bail. Where had he been going? Why had there been so elaborate a further deception, with the bogus Karim Ali living in Manners Deep? Where was the true Karim Ali now, where the imposter and his companions? . . . A general call to all police stations, ports, and airports had gone out; detain Karim Ali, his wife, and his companions. They had photographs of the real Karim Ali, so that he could be clearly identified. But what did the bogus Karim Ali normally look like? Since his impersonation had been so good, he must resemble the genuine man, but it probably wouldn't be difficult for him to look quite different, except to a trained observer. And as for the other people with the exception of the man he'd met and Mrs Ali, if she was Mrs Ali, they only had Judy's and Nick's descriptions to go on and these, understandably, were not good.

He suddenly smacked his right fist into the palm of his left hand in an unusual gesture of irritation. What were the answers to all the questions?

The Ransomes didn't quite know how to view events. Nick had told them that there'd been a bit of a bother, but had been vague when it came to details. Then Judy had turned up and had given a more dramatic version of events. And finally, the detective inspector and detective sergeant called to question both Judy and Nick.

In the kitchen, Ben said: 'If you ask me, we haven't heard a quarter of what went on!' He crossed to the stove, picked up the coffee-pot, and refilled their two cups.

Caroline's expression became even more worried. 'I think we ought to get on to Thelma this time.'

'And tell her what? That there's been some sort of trouble, but we don't really know anything beyond the fact that Nick drove a car through a pair of gates at a speed Judy conservatively estimates at a hundred and fifty! Can you imagine how Thelma will react to that?'

'Yes, I can,' she replied unhappily.

'Then if you'll take my advice, you'll leave it to the two of them to explain things to their respective parents.'

'That's being – well, cowardly.'

'There are times when it's a positive virtue to be a coward.'

'The trouble is . . . I'm sure Judy will manage everything perfectly, but Nick's not nearly so good at that sort of thing.'

In the sitting-room, Basdon said: 'Well, that seems to have covered everything. Thanks for all your help.' He stood. 'There's just one thing I'd like to say . . .' He stopped, shook his head. 'Let's leave it unsaid.'

Johns shut his notebook and reached out for the cup of coffee to drain it.

'D'you think you'll catch them?' Nick asked.

'There's every chance,' replied Basdon, trying to sound more confident than he felt. Their best chance had been in the first few hours; by now, the gang would have gone to earth and it could prove a very difficult job to dig them out.

'By the way,' Judy said, 'there's something I've forgotten until now to tell you.'

Basdon sat down once more.

'Just before we left the house, we saw Mrs Ali trying to make a telephone call and from the way she acted it seemed to me she was asking someone what the number was and then writing it down. So when we were in the kitchen, I went over to see what she'd written and I tore off the top sheet on the message pad.'

'So that's why you acted so stupidly!' exclaimed Nick.

'I was not being stupid. I've just explained that.'

'You haven't realised that the time you wasted meant the man came into the kitchen and saw us?'

'It was all a question of priorities,' she said loftily. She produced a scrumpled piece of paper and handed this to Basdon. 'This could be very important, couldn't it?'

Basdon, trying to be tactful, made a sound which left it unclear with which viewpoint he agreed. He smoothed out the paper. 'It certainly could be a telephone number and with a string of figures this long it'll be an international one. We'll check it out.' He folded the paper and put it in his wallet, then stood once more.

Johns entered Basdon's office. 'It's a telephone number, all right. 010 is the international exchange, 34 is Spain, 972 is the province of Gerona, and 4504603 is a number in Castillo Blanco. Incidentally, if I've got it right, you leave the 9 out if you dial from here.'

'Where's that?'

'On the coast, between Barcelona and the French frontier. It's a development especially for boat enthusiasts; plenty of canals so you can tie up your boat at the bottom of the garden . . . When I'm rich, that's where I'm going to buy a house.'

'I thought it was to be a place like Manners Deep . . . You know the recipe for tiger soup, don't you? It starts, first catch your tiger. Have you an identification on the owner of the house?'

'His name's Ahmed Kayyal.'

'Sounds as if it could be Arabic again.' Basdon began to fidget with a pencil. 'How do we proceed from here, remembering it could have been a straightforward call to friends?'

100

'At a time when the house was in turmoil because their two captives had escaped?'

'People act so illogically that it's no good believing you'll always find logic in what they do.'

'Judy is quite certain the call was important and when Mrs Ali didn't get an answer she was very disturbed. That suggests it had a connection with what was happening.'

'And I'd suggest that Judy and Nick were both in the kind of state where we can't rely on any emotional judgement they made.'

Johns was familiar with Basdon's method of testing a proposition by acting as devil's advocate; he waited.

'I think you're probably right, however. But we must make certain that the Spanish police realise the enquiries need to be very discreet because at this stage we cannot be certain that the people in that house have anything at all to do with the case.'

The message was received on Sunday afternoon. Enquiries had been made in Castillo Blanco. Ahmed Kayyal, owner of number 31, Estropoñas, was seldom in residence; perhaps as little as a fortnight a year. A security firm were contracted to keep watch on the place and they said that no one had been there for the past six months. Kayyal was an elderly man, married with either two or three wives. He owned a two-masted schooner which normally was only berthed there when he was in residence. According to records, he had never caused the slightest trouble.

'That would seem to be the end of that, then,' said Basdon.

'Looks like it, sir.'

Basdon yawned. He checked the time. 'I was meant to take the wife to visit some of her relations today. When I told her I'd got to come into the office this morning after all, the only way I could keep the peace was to promise to be back home just as soon as was humanly possible, so I'd better get moving.' He stood. 'You know, I'd give a lot to be certain exactly where Karim Ali is at this precise moment.'

101

Basdon's question was answered on the following Monday morning. Detective Sergeant Stevens, a member of the Special Branch on routine embassy watch, saw the man come through the main doorway of the Shishanna Embassy and walk unevenly across the lawn. His hair was thick, black, and slightly curly, his beard full, his cheekbones high, his nose hooked, and his lips thick; his right leg was in plaster. With the sun full on his face, the neat surgical patch on his right cheek was very obvious; less obvious, but visible, was the bruising which extended beyond the patch on one side.

Johns looked across the sitting-room of Fawver Cottage, first at Judy, then at Nick. 'So that's how things are. The genuine Karim Ali is at the Shishanna Embassy and almost certainly was taken there after the car accident so that he could be treated by a doctor. The bogus Karim Ali, together with his accomplices, quit Manners Deep the moment it was obvious that you'd escaped. And, frankly, we've no idea where they are now.

'All the time Karim Ali stays within the embassy enclosure, there is nothing we can do – as you'll probably know, that's extra-territorial ground. Of course, if he tries to leave, we'll arrest him.'

'But surely he's got to leave some time?' said Judy.

'As to that, people have stayed in embassies in other countries for years in order to avoid being arrested. But he probably hopes that fairly soon we'll tire of watching and then he'll be able to slide out and escape.'

'And will you tire?'

He smiled briefly. 'That's right outside my province. Thank goodness!'

'There's still something I don't understand.'

'Which is what?'

'Why should he hold up in the embassy when that means he's virtually imprisoned there?'

'He went there because it was the only place where he could receive any medical treatment without subsequently being

102

arrested for breaking the terms of his bail.'

She looked as if about to say something more, but then remained silent.

'There's something odd about that, isn't there?' said Nick uncertainly. 'I mean, Karim Ali's an Iranian. So why did he go to the Shishanna Embassy? And why are they protecting him?'

'I'm sorry, but I can't answer because I just don't know.'

'It could be important,' said Judy.

'I don't think so, not in practical terms.'

'You mean, simply from the point of view of arresting him?'

'That's right.'

'And no one can be bothered to look beyond the obvious?'

Her aggressive persistence made him wonder if she had some vague, instinctive knowledge of the politics which lay behind this case; then he realised that this was most unlikely and the cause was far more probably the fact that she was of a very determined character and liked to have everything cut and dried.

'Well?' she prompted.

He spoke with undiminished good humour. 'I'm only a lowly detective sergeant. I don't make the policies, but just do as I'm told.'

' "Theirs not to reason why"?'

He looked blankly at her.

'Longfellow,' said Nick.

'Tennyson,' she corrected scathingly.

Johns stood. He admired Judy, but truth to tell found her very difficult in her present mood. 'I'll be on my way . . .'

She interrupted him. 'What's happening about the telephone number?'

'I think I mentioned that that's been checked. The number is of a house belonging to an elderly Arab who's hardly ever around. He isn't there now.'

'You didn't explain why Mrs Ali expected someone to be there and why it was so important.'

'Let's be fair. You can't be certain on either of those points.'

'Yes, I can. We'd just broken free and so they had to catch us or obviously their plans would be bust wide open. D'you think Mrs Ali would ever have chosen a time like that to make a social call? And if it wasn't social, then obviously it was important; and if it was important, equally obviously she expected someone to be there.'

'There might just be something in that if you'd any proof that the number written down on the pad was the number she tried to dial.'

'She's hardly likely to have written it down if she wasn't going to use it.'

Johns finally allowed his exasperation to show. 'All we know for certain is that there's no one living in the house right now, there hasn't been for months, and there's nothing to suggest that there's likely to be in the near future.'

'Does that mean you're not going to check again?'

'To what purpose?'

'Because it's very important.'

'How?'

'I don't know; I only know it is.'

Nick, who was becoming embarrassed by her aggressive manner, tried to introduce a touch of lightness. 'That sounds somewhat illogical!'

'Illogicality is in the ears of the listener,' she snapped.

'Well, my ears are beginning to burn from what my detective inspector's probably saying because I'm not yet back at the grindstone.' Johns then added, speaking more to Nick than to Judy: 'I reckon the two of you were lucky, but you wouldn't have been lucky if you hadn't had a hell of a lot of courage to back it up.' His tone was unmistakably sincere.

Nick went with Johns out to the latter's car. Johns opened the driving door, half turned. 'If you'll take my advice, Nick, you'll stop worrying about everything. It'll make life much easier.' It was obvious that he hoped his words would be passed on to Judy. 'Well, so long.' He smiled, sat down behind the wheel, pulled the door shut, started the engine, and drove off, waving once as he pulled away from the grass verge.

Nick slowly returned into the house. Judy was still in the sitting-room and as he entered she said heatedly: 'They're so thick! Of course the number was important, of course Mrs Ali believed there'd be someone there, of course it's got something to do with all that's happened.'

'But he was right to this extent, you can't . . .'

'Don't *you* start telling me what I can't do.'

'I wouldn't dare.'

She stared at him, then suddenly laughed. 'Have I been sounding that bad?'

'Worse.'

'But it's so frustrating when I know it's so important.' She fiddled with a curl of hair, looked briefly at him. 'Whereabouts in Spain did he say the house was?'

'Wasn't the place something like Castle Blank?'

'That's it – Castillo Blanco. You really are hopeless at languages.'

'I like that! At least I had a rough idea, which is more than you did.'

She ignored that. She continued to fiddle with her hair. 'If we were there . . .'

She became silent.

'If we were at the North Pole, we could talk to the penguins.'

'South Pole. Don't you know anything?'

'North or South, what's the difference?'

'A lot, to anyone who's concerned about the facts . . . Nick . . .' She looked at him again, this time with studied casualness. 'I've been thinking. We really do need a break after all we've been through. Don't you agree?'

'But isn't being here instead of at home really a break . . .' He stopped as belatedly, he realised the significance of her question. 'If you're suggesting . . .'

'Talking about Castillo Blanco reminded me that friends of Mother bought a house there towards the end of last year.'

'Bully for them. But if you reckon . . .'

'I know they'd be only too glad to have us stay.'

'No.'

'Wouldn't you love to be down there, in the sun, swimming, windsurfing, water-skiing?'

'That's not why you want to go. And if you think Mum and Dad would agree, knowing what's happened, you've got another think coming.'

She had been speaking in honeyed tones, since she wanted him to agree to her suggestion, but now her voice appreciably sharpened. 'For Pete's sake, you can't be that soft. You don't tell them about all that's happened.'

He spoke uncomfortably. 'They've a nasty habit of finding out the truth.'

'Only because you're mentally transparent. But since you are, I'll do the asking and I'll guarantee they won't suspect a thing.'

'I wouldn't be so sure about that. And another thing, there's no way they can begin to afford my fare.'

'I'll tell Mother she's paying for both of us.'

'Just like that?'

'That's right.'

'It's crazy. After all, if the police say there's nothing to be done . . .'

'Nick, you've got things the wrong way round. All right, I wouldn't mind finding out if anyone does turn up at that house, just to satisfy my curiosity, but the reason for suggesting we go down there is that I really do need a complete break from everything that's gone on here. And it'll be ten times nicer with you because you're so alive and such fun to be with.'

She spoke with such flattering sincerity that he found himself beginning to believe her. And yet he knew she was lying . . .

The air stewardess walked slowly down the aisle of the Boeing 727, checking that all passengers had fastened their seat-belts. After she'd passed, Nick looked out through the rain-speckled porthole at the grey-bellied clouds which promised much heavier rain. But in two hours, more or less, the plane would be landing in brilliant sunshine . . .

The engines' notes rose in pitch and the plane began to move forward along the feeder in the direction of the runway. He turned to glance at Judy, to see if she was sharing his excitement, but she was reading a magazine. Constant travel had made her blasé. He looked out once more. According to something he'd read, a jet plane taking off developed roughly the same acceleration as a Formula One car . . .

Chapter 16

The sun blazed down from a cloudless sky and only the slight sea breeze brought any relief from the heat. On the wide belt of sand which stretched the whole length of the very wide bay, thousands of tourists sun-bathed, many of them risking quite serious burns. Out at sea, windsurfers and yachts made the best they could of the fickle and fitful breeze, and power-boats, towing water-skiiers, left creamy wakes.

Twenty years before, Castillo Blanco had been a marsh, often partially inundated in winter storms, visited only by wildfowlers; now it was an *urbanización* expressly for boat enthusiasts. Two main wide channels and many side ones had been constructed, together with two large basins which could accommodate yachts unable to sail up the channels. There were four large pyramidal blocks of apartments situated on the front, but otherwise there were only houses which ranged from small, inexpensive semi-detacheds to very large, luxurious and expensive villas. Twenty kilometers away were the foothills of the Pyrenees, looking in the early morning or the evening, when the air was still and relatively cool, as if they were at less than half the distance.

Judy and Nick braked their bicycles to a halt. 'That must be the house,' she said.

They stared across the road. Immediately to the right of a rectangular inlet – this provided moorings for boats under seven metres which belonged to people whose homes did not front water – was a very large, ranch-style house built on three plots. A high wall ran round the three land sides. A number of cypresses grew to the right of the house and amongst these could be seen the top two steps of a diving-board.

'Every shutter's closed,' said Judy, her disappointment

obvious. 'It doesn't look as if anyone can be here.'

'You knew there wasn't before we came.'

'Nothing of the sort. All I knew was that no one answered the telephone.'

He didn't argue any further. Sometimes it was impossible to get her to accept any logic other than her own.

'They must arrive soon.'

'And if they don't?'

'I tell you I'm right, I know I am!' She turned, and when she saw his expression she smiled. 'What's more, I know just what you're thinking. I'm being impossible. Right?'

'Who am I to argue with you?'

'I'm sorry.' She sounded sincere. 'But I was so certain . . .' She looked back at the house as if, as had happened to Sleeping Beauty, the scene would suddenly return to life. 'Oh, well, there's no point in hanging around here. Are you thirsty?'

'Dehydrated.'

'Then let's go and get something to drink. And then why don't we hire one of those Hobbycats? It'll be lovely sailing on a day like this if we can find some wind.'

As he mounted his bike and followed her, he wondered whether she'd finally accepted the fact that there was nothing more they could do?

Judy insisted on visually checking on the house each day, but Nick became certain that this had become no more than a routine chore, carried out only because she was so stubborn. As soon as it was obvious the shutters were still closed and the padlocks were on the two sets of gates, she was the first to suggest they go swimming, sailing, windsurfing, snorkeling, or water-skiing.

On Sunday afternoon they swam and then lay on the sand, sun-bathing, drifting into and out of sleep . . .

'I suppose we ought to go and check,' said Judy.

'Today's Sunday. A day of rest. Forget it.'

'Come on, it's good for the soul to have to do something.'

'Maybe good for yours, but fatal for mine.'

'You're just decadently sybaritic.'

'Couldn't agree more if that means I prefer snoozing in the sun to cycling miles to look at an unoccupied house.'

But for the need to show him she was made of sterner stuff, she might have forgone her duty and continued to lie in the luxuriously warm sunshine, but as it was she badgered him into getting up and walking back to where they'd left their bicycles, carefully padlocked to a lamp-post. They cycled slowly down to one of the main roads which traversed the *urbanización* longitudinally, then turned right into the labyrinth of side roads in Estropoñas, one of the five zones into which the *urbanización* was divided for administrative purposes.

As they came in sight of number 31, the first things they noticed were the two masts which towered above the roofline; the second, that most of the shutters were now open.

'What did I tell you!' she said excitedly.

'The fact that someone's living there now doesn't prove anything,' he replied.

'It proves I'm right.'

'According to you, what doesn't?'

She looked from one end of the grounds to the other. 'I can't see anyone around. How are we going to find out who's there?'

'I don't know. Any more than what we do after that. I mean, so the owner's turned up with a few of his wives and a yacht. So what?'

'You can't really be that thick. We find out why Mrs Ali tried to phone him, of course.'

'I suppose you'll march in and ask him?'

'If I have to, I will.'

'You'll be on your own.'

'Coward.'

'Just cautious. I've had all the excitement I want for a very long time. Look, Judy, if you feel you must do something, get on the phone to Sergeant Johns and tell him the owner's arrived and if he rings up . . .'

'Mike said we can borrow the boat any time we want.'

'Which has nothing to do with . . .'

110

'There's no way they can prevent a boat sailing along after dark.'

'No!'

'Nick, it's not like you to be so chicken-hearted.'

'Maybe I'm learning sense in my old age.'

'But surely you want to find out what's really been going on?'

'No.'

'I don't believe you.' She studied the house closely. 'It's bound to be easy from the water.'

'Forget it.'

'Where's your spirit of adventure?'

'Left behind in England.'

'Just this once . . .'

'I am not sailing Mike's boat down in a crazy attempt to find out who's living in that house.'

As he throttled back, so that the dory with cathedral-shaped hull did not exceed the speed limit of five knots, Nick wondered whether he needed to see a psychiatrist? Despite all his firm, unshakable decisions, here he was, sailing towards the house belonging to Kayyal . . .

The moon gave enough light for them to be able to sail without using the small spotlight. He saw the channel to port, throttled back still further, turned. Now, they could just make out the schooner, her masts, in the soft, diffused light, seemingly stretching right up into the night sky.

He said to Judy: 'We'll go right past. With any luck, they'll be sitting out on the patio or lawn.'

'I'm sure they will be.'

He looked at her quickly, his attention caught by an unusual inflection in her voice, but her expression told him nothing. Just so long as she remembered that, no matter what happened, they were not setting one foot ashore . . .

The schooner was made fast alongside the metre-high bank; she was in complete darkness and as they slid past, there was no sign of life on deck. Beyond her, the grounds also were in darkness and only the house was illuminated. Astern of her was a boat-house, which had not been visible from the road, providing a wet berth.

'I can hear them,' she said.

The voices reached them as a low murmur, without intonations, so that it was impossible to judge what language was being spoken. At least half-a-dozen people, he guessed.

They passed the end of the grounds to reach the inlet. He increased the revs. 'I'll turn, then sail back as slowly as possible, but I must keep some way on her in order to steer . . . If there's still no one outside, that'll be all we can do.'

'I wonder if anyone's on the yacht?'

'I doubt it.'

'But just go a bit closer, in case.'

He made a wide circle, then headed down the channel. They drew level with the northern end of the grounds.

'Closer,' she said.

'What's the point if no one's outside?' Nevertheless, he closed the bank.

They passed the boat-house and he put on slight port helm to take them clear of the schooner's bows. They sailed the length of her. 'Nick, go alongside the bank.'

'No.'

'But all I want to do is stand and listen in case I can hear something that's important. That can't possibly do any harm, can it?'

He hesitated, decided he really was being rather silly. Since there was no one in the garden, where was the harm? He steered into the bank, the outboard in neutral.

Judy reached out and grabbed a tyre, lying against the concrete wall of the bank as a fender, and pulled them alongside. 'You'll have to turn the engine off.'

He wondered if anyone in the house would mark that the outboard had stopped and question why, decided it was very unlikely; even though it was dark, the sound of an outboard was surely too commonplace to have caught their attention in the first place. He switched off, then used a handy rope, looped through a tyre, as a temporary mooring.

They could now hear the voices clearly enough to be certain they were not speaking English; Arabic, Nick thought, remembering how that language had sounded.

'Give me your shoulder,' she whispered.

He braced himself. The boat rocked and for a moment her fingers dug into his shoulder, then she established her balance. 'Can you see anyone now?' he asked.

'There's definitely no one outside the house. They must all be in one of the middle rooms; I think I can hear the clink of knives and forks . . . There's a woman just come in sight of one of the windows . . . She seems to be serving something. If only we could see them now, when they're eating and too busy to worry about anything else . . .'

He realised he should have been prepared for her next move; knowing her as well as he did, it really was predictable. But, mentally dulled by the warmth and sense of timelessness which water induced, he was caught totally off guard when she let go of his shoulder and, using the tyre as a stepping-stone, climbed fleetly up over the edge of the bank.

He stood hurriedly and the boat rocked so violently that he had to reach for support. 'Come on back down,' he whispered urgently.

'Stop panicking. I told you, they're eating and can't possibly notice me.'

'You promised you wouldn't try anything like this.'

'I had my fingers crossed.' She chuckled as she moved away, making little or no noise on the grass.

He wished he could let her go on her own so that if she ran into trouble she'd have only herself to blame, but knew he couldn't. He secured the mooring more firmly, then climbed up on to the bank.

The lawn sloped gradually upwards so that the house stood about a metre and a half higher than the bank; the trees cast shadows which in places merged into darkness. Most of the shutters of the bottom windows were open and light spilled out on to the grass and he caught sight of her as she moved to

113

her right to skirt one of these patches. He was about to go forward when it seemed to him that there had been movement away to the right. He concentrated on that point, but could make out nothing, so he used the old dodge of concentrating on a spot to the side. A few seconds later, he became certain that there was something there.

He knew the familiar sense of tension and excitement which dried the throat and sent the heart thumping. Had he seen an animal – a stray dog – which posed no threat to Judy, or . . . There was further movement and just for a second a man was visible before he slipped into shadows and the darkness closed over him once more.

Nick now knew fear.

Chapter 17

The man was stalking Judy and she was totally unaware of the fact. So unaware that now she was standing to the side of one window and staring inside, careless that sufficient light was suffusing sideways to make her visible to anyone outside.

Nick's first reaction was to shout a warning. But he realised that that would startle her and therefore her reactions would be delayed; should she recover less quickly than her pursuer, this could prove fatal. He had to find some other way of helping her. He moved carefully forward, knowing that any sound could prove disastrous, but that any delay must be fatal.

The distance between himself and the man shortened, but not by as much as the distance between the man and Judy. Desperate to find some way of safely warning her, he even tried telepathy, but she stayed where she was, staring intently into the dining-room.

The man approached the light and for the first time Nick realised that he was carrying a knife. Fresh fear forced Nick to move too quickly and his foot knocked into something that skittered sideways, to the accompaniment of a sharp sound. The man stopped, turned, and looked back. Nick held his head forward and down so that his face was hidden as far as possible, knowing how that could show up. He waited until the added tension became too great, then looked up. The man, obviously having dismissed the noise as of no consequence to himself, had resumed his stalk. And now that he was close to Judy, he held the knife slightly ahead of himself at waist level, in the classic position of attack.

Whatever Nick's foot had struck, had been solid. He bent down and his fingers touched a stone, some six to seven

115

centimetres in diameter, heavy enough to be used as a missile . . .

The man was now close to Judy. And, as if she finally sensed his presence, she suddenly turned. She saw him. Recognising there was no further need for secrecy, he raced forward, shouting as he did so.

At the end of the previous summer term, Nick's sports report had referred to him as an erratic cricketer, capable but often careless through inattention; the report had, however, added that when concentrating, his fielding had been excellent, particularly his returns to the wicket . . . With far more at stake than running out one of the other side's batsmen, Nick took aim and threw.

The stone hit the man on the side of his temple. He gasped, dropped the knife, clapped his hand to his head and staggered sideways, weak-kneed but not actually falling.

Judy whirled round and raced towards the edge of the lawn. As Nick followed her, he heard someone call out from the house. They jumped down into the boat. Nick went to untie the rope looped through the tyre, but either because he'd used a wrong knot or because his fingers had become all thumbs, he could not free it.

'Hurry,' said Judy urgently.

As a last resort, he tugged violently and one end came free. He whipped this through the tyre, pushed them away from the bank. Since they'd tied up beam on, they didn't make much way, but as the two pursuers reached the bank and stood there, it became clear they'd gone far enough. He pressed the self-starter button and the engine fired. He engaged drive and steered for the middle of the channel.

'I'm . . . I'm sorry,' she said.

Anger – as much from fear on her behalf as anything – made him say sharply: 'That man could have killed you.'

'Only if you hadn't been there.' She reached over and lightly touched his arm in a familiar gesture, then sat back. 'Guess who was in the house.'

'I'm not in a fit state to guess anything.'

'Karim Ali.'

'Who? Come off it, that's impossible. The police must still be watching the embassy grounds, so he couldn't have got free.'

'Karim Ali, the genuine Karim Ali, is in that house. You can see a fresh scar on his cheek and there are still traces of heavy bruising.'

'But how could he have broken out of the embassy?'

'Think. He didn't.'

'But you've just said . . .'

'After the car crash, they smuggled him on to the yacht, despite his injuries which needed medical attention; maybe they found a doctor in France who was willing to go out to the yacht and attend him and not ask questions. The bogus Karim Ali escaped from Manners Deep and he'd have realised that once the police had learned what had happened, they'd know that if they moved quickly enough they could possibly still catch the genuine Karim Ali before he reached whatever sanctuary he was heading for. So the bogus one slipped into the embassy and once again impersonated the genuine one, only this time sporting injuries to make it appear he *had* been in a car accident instead of doing everything possible to make it seem he hadn't. That way, the police would not start searching for the real man outside the country.'

She must be right, he thought. Not only did it make sense, this plan showed the same brazen daring which had distinguished the first one . . . His thoughts were interrupted as an engine barked into life. He looked astern and saw a large ski-boat, bows already rising, round the schooner. That ski-boat had come from the boathouse, he thought, as he pushed the hand throttle to maximum setting. In the brief second before their own engine responded with screaming power, he saw a column of water rise to starboard. That had been a shot! Then their bows lifted and they were pressed back into their seats and within seconds were approaching the main channel. He put the helm over, but had greatly underestimated their

117

speed and the dory 'skidded' as she turned and for one agonising moment it seemed they must crash into the bank. Then they just skimmed it.

They swept into the main channel, heeling heavily and churning the water white. He should have slacked off the helm; now they were committed to turning a full circle.

The pursuing helmsman was far more skilful. He'd slowed and started to turn early and so had kept the boat under full control. The second it was possible, he went on to full throttle, aiming the bows just ahead of the dory.

There were two stabs of light, but the sounds of the shots were lost in the roar of the outboards. One bullet missed, the other pierced the hull of the dory just above the waterline on the starboard side and exited just under the waterline on the port side. A thin jet of water sprayed inboard.

It was obvious that the helmsman of the ski-boat was going to try to ram them, a surer method of attack than shooting when the violent motions of the boats made aiming a matter of luck not judgement. The ski-boat was much heavier and faster, Nick thought grimly, so in this deadly game of dodgems, almost all the advantages were with the pursuers; perhaps their only one was a greater manoeuvrability. But even this advantage would be lost if he made another mistake like the one of a moment before.

The ski-boat was now trying to box them in, forcing them so close to the bank that they no longer had the room to turn; then, they could be rammed with ease. Their only chance of escaping this was to come round the ski-boat's stern; but the helmsman would be expecting such a move . . .

He waited until they were within seconds of a direct collision, then throttled back sharply. Almost immediately, the bows of the ski-boat dropped slightly and came round more sharply to port to maintain collision course. Immediately, he made no further move, hoping this would give the impression that he'd been mesmerised by fear. Then, at the last split second, he swung the helm over to starboard and slammed the throttle wide open. The boat heeled over so violently that

Judy fell on to him, but he used the wheel to hold himself steady. They skimmed past the stern of the ski-boat, with little more than a canvas to spare.

The helmsman of the ski-boat sharply tightened his turning circle to follow them round and advanced to full power. The ski-boat heeled, completely ruining the aim of one of the gunmen who had been about to fire at a range so close that even allowing for conditions it would have been difficult not to have hit the dory again. In the event, the bullet went skywards.

Desperately, Nick tried to work out what to do. Because the ski-boat was faster, there could be no direct escape; because it was heavier, any collision would be fatal to the dory; and although the dory had proved to be slightly more manoeuvrable, the difference was not so great as he had at first hoped . . .

They thrashed their way down channel, at a speed many times the legal maximum, their violent wake sending moored boats pitching and tugging at their ropes. A slight bend became a hazard that called for all the skill he could muster . . .

'Where are they?' he shouted, not daring to look back.

She had to put her mouth so close to his ear that strands of her hair tickled his cheek. 'Not very far and gaining fast.'

Now they could see the floodlit Club Nautico – a building designed to resemble the bridge of a ship – the customs post, and the sea beyond. There were no more side channels and he realised that unwittingly he had landed them in a trap. He could not turn back without slowing right down, which would leave them wide open to being rammed, yet to continue out to sea would leave them at a fatal disadvantage because of their slower speed.

'They're not getting any closer now,' Judy shouted.

They wouldn't, he thought. They were the wolf, shepherding the sheep towards its destruction . . .

They roared past the customs post, a small, square building, brightly illuminated, with on the right a large sign in four languages which said that any incoming boat from abroad must report and make a full declaration and that the maximum speed from that point in was five knots. What were the *guardia* going to make of two boats passing them at many times the legal maximum . . .?

In the subdued moonlight, the sea appeared to be as flat calm as it had been that afternoon, but in fact there was now a swell. Because of their speed, they began to pitch heavily, sending sheets of spray rocketing aft to slam into and over the windscreen.

'You've got to go faster,' she shouted.

The outboard was at full revs. In any case, the movements of the dory were already dangerously violent.

He looked back and was shocked to see how close the ski-boat now was; only seconds before the bows would crush into them, probably rolling them over . . . He put on starboard helm and they came round hard, so hard that the gunwale dipped until, for one long second, water poured inboard. Then the gunwale rose clear and they were heading back towards land. He saw the ski-boat come round, aiming to use its extra speed to cut them off so that they had to head back to sea, where they could more easily be murdered . . .

He'd fooled them once and gone round their stern. They'd probably expect him to try the same manoeuvre again. He throttled back, then put the helm to starboard and, after a couple of seconds, advanced the throttle. As the helmsman of the ski-boat altered course to prevent them escaping past the stern, he swung the wheel to port. By the time the other could react, they were on a course that must take them clear. Two shots were fired. It was impossible to guess where the bullets went.

Now the dory was heading directly towards the main channel and Nick reckoned that the distance was still such that it was touch-and-go whether he could make it it before the ski-boat caught up. But even if he succeeded in making it first, what then? Where could there be any safety from men who were determined to kill them, regardless of the consequences? Or, more probably, were confident that they would be able to escape any consequences.

However hard the windscreen wiper worked, it couldn't counter the heavy spray, and the screen was constantly rendered virtually opaque. But it was during one brief moment of clarity that he saw two figures, in uniform, outside the customs post. And into his mind flashed the question he'd put to himself earlier on. What would the *guardia* think when the speed limit was ignored so flagrantly and so comprehensively? The answer was obvious. They'd want to question the helmsmen. And they were armed with semi-automatic rifles . . .

'Grab something and hold tight,' he shouted. 'I'm running ashore.'

She braced herself.

He aimed to the right of the channel and kept his mental fingers crossed that at this point the sand shelved gently. The ski-boat's helmsman, thinking he was making an error of judgement, concentrated on cutting him off from the channel entrance . . .

Despite the fact that he cut the throttle when still a way out, they hit the sand with enough force to jerk them heavily forward. Their world turned into a chaos of spray and jolting movement which threatened to shake the dory apart. Then there was one last thump and they came to an abrupt stop. The two *guardia* raced towards them, rifles unslung. Three hundred metres off-shore, the ski-boat turned to port and left at full speed.

Chapter 18

Judy's mother owned a large and luxurious flat in Abbots Lane, in Knightsbridge, and Judy and Nick both stayed there Tuesday night, on their return from Spain.

The following morning, Detective Sergeant Straw called at twenty past ten.

He was very earnest-looking and he frowned a lot when he concentrated, so that first impressions were that he was of a very serious nature; only after a while did it become obvious that in some measure appearances were deceptive and that although he had a serious side, he also had a good sense of humour. He sat in one of the chairs in the sitting-room, rather worried that something so slender might not carry his weight. 'I understand that the two of you have had a bit of a hectic time in Spain?'

'It had its moments,' Judy replied.

He looked at her, surprised by her cool manner. He cleared his throat. 'I've been asked to come along and explain to you what's been happening.'

Judy, in an irritating tone, said: 'We know what's been happening. After all, it's been happening to us.'

'Er . . . Yes . . . I suppose I should have said, to explain *why* it's been happening.'

'That's simple. Because no one would believe Nick.'

Straw spoke quickly. 'I expect you've read or heard something about the Middle East country, Shishanna? How oil was found there and a primitive place suddenly became exceedingly wealthy and in consequence set out on a spending spree?'

'Yes, we have.'

'Then you probably also realise that when the price of oil

began to fall, the sultan suddenly found himself in severe financial trouble. In consequence of this, a great deal of the construction work was halted and this led to unemployement, especially amongst migrant workers; on top of this, the sultan decided to introduce a tax system, something which hadn't been known before. It's a fact of human nature that when people enjoy luxuries for any length of time, they begin to see them not as luxuries but as necessities . . .' He came to a stop, noticing the look of ironic amusement on Judy's face. He flushed. Perhaps he had begun to sound rather pompous . . . 'Anyway, people became discontented and there was lots of talk of revolution.

'The sultan realised that if he was to stay in power he had to find a way of replacing the oil revenues and using that money to keep the people quiet. And to cut a long story short, he decided that the only thing which could offer the enormous profits he needed was drugs.

'It was easy enough to import the raw materials and set up refineries; as sultan, he merely gave the orders. The difficulty came in exporting the drugs into consuming countries. That's when the sultan decided on using diplomatic bags. You must know that the term means anything from a small parcel to a huge packing case which is allowed to enter a country without being examined – each country is supposed to be on its honour not to import anything which shouldn't be imported.

'Drugs came into this country in the Shishanna diplomatic bags. Now, there was the problem of selling the drugs to the main distributors. The real trouble here was the risk of one of the distributors being caught and admitting to the source of the drugs. Such a revelation would blacken the sultan's character – and apparently he's a very vain man who likes to believe that everyone respects him – but more importantly, diplomatic steps would be taken to bring the traffic to an abrupt halt.

'The way they set out to deal with this problem was to find a middleman, who apparently had no connection with Shishanna, who would appear to be the principal and sell to

123

the distributors. He'd be paid a very high commission because it was understood that if ever he were caught, he'd never tell the truth. That middleman was Karim Sayyid ibn Ali.

'Ali worked the racket successfully until bad luck had him caught in Manchester. And then, even though he'd only been arrested on a relatively minor charge because the police couldn't get sufficient evidence against him, he told his employers that if he were ever actually imprisoned he was going to expose them, so they'd better find some way of keeping him free. And if they thought murdering him was the easiest way, he'd arranged for all the details to be sent to the British government in the event of his death.

'This left the sultan of Shishanna in a fix. It was clear that if nothing was done, Ali was almost certain to be jailed. The embassy tried to bring pressure on the government to have Ali discharged from the case, but that sort of thing's impossible here. So then they had to get him out of the country before the trial. But he was a marked man after appearing before the magistrates and any attempt to leave the country by normal routes was bound to lead to disaster. He'd be recognised and since he'd have broken one of the conditions of bail, from then on he'd be held in custody. And the moment that happened, he was going to spill the beans. That left only one thing to do – to spirit him out of this country and into another.

'They decided to smuggle him out in a yacht; if you arrange things well, it's not all that difficult to take off from some deserted part of the coast and rendezvous with a yacht. It was agreed to take him to Spain. He wasn't going to risk Shishanna for obvious reasons and Iran is no good to him with the present regime in power – and most other countries have extradition treaties with Britain. But at the time of planning, Spain didn't have any such treaty and even if one was later introduced – as it has just been – under Spanish law, a punitive enactment cannot be retrospectively applied so he'd be safe.

'One of the conditions of his bail was that he had to report to the local police station three times a week. This meant there were never more than two clear days open to him, so everything had to be very carefully organised. If anything was suspected while the yacht were still in British waters, he was for the high jump; even if the yacht reached international waters, the British authorities might find some way of boarding it and arresting him.

'You'll have guessed how they set about things. A man who looked very much like Ali was to impersonate him. When this imposter was due to report to the police station, he'd claim to be ill. A policeman would be detailed to visit him and he'd make certain the lighting was poor so that any slight differences in appearance would be lost.

'On the nineteenth of last month, Ali was due to leave Manners Deep and board the waiting yacht; the imposter, who over the weeks had learned to impersonate Ali even to the extent of trimming his hair and beard exactly in Ali's fashion, was to take his place . . . Everything worked until the fog rolled in. Then a short journey turned into a long one, the driver hurried too much, knowing the time of the rendezvous was important, and the car skidded off the road. Ali was injured and knocked unconscious. The driver, panicking, rushed off to ring through to Manners Deep to report the disaster and whilst he was gone, Nick turned up.

'Somone – almost certainly the bogus Ali – obviously can think very fast. He decided that the only way in which there was a chance of saving the situation, which meant keeping everything quiet until the injured Ali had arrived in Spain, was to scotch any possibility that he'd been in the crash . . . The rest you know.'

Judy broke the short silence. 'And it all very nearly succeeded. Because, as I said before, no one was prepared to believe Nick.'

'You know, it can be very difficult when all the evidence seems to point . . .'

'It's very difficult, yes, when one has no imagination.'

Straw said nothing. His detective inspector had impressed on him the need to be diplomatic.

125

Nick said curiously: 'What would have happened if we hadn't gone to Spain?'

'Then the bogus Ali would have shed his disguise and slipped out of the embassy as soon as it was known that the genuine Ali was safely in Spain.'

'Leaving a mystery,' said Judy, 'which no one would ever have solved.'

'I'm sure we'd have done so.'

'On past evidence, I very much doubt it.'

Straw thought of an answer, but regretfully reminded himself that he musn't make it. He stood. 'I'll be leaving . . .'

'There is one more thing,' said Nick.

'What's that?'

'What happens now to Karim Ali – has he escaped scot-free?'

'I suppose the answer to that is, yes and no. For the moment, yes. But if he leaves Spain, he won't ever be allowed back in. And under a new law, the authorities there can expel anyone they've good reason to believe is of an undesirable character. We're making certain the authorities are under no illusions about what sort of character he really is. So long-term, no, he hasn't escaped scot-free.' He waited, but when Nick remained silent, he said goodbye, left.

Nick looked across at Judy. 'You were a bit sharp on him, weren't you?'

'With every justification. If the police had had the sense to believe you earlier on, they'd have realised in time what was happening.'

'But fair's fair, it was difficult for them . . .'

'Nonsense.'

Prudence entered the room. 'I heard the policeman leave,' she said, in her soft, far-away voice which so often suggested that she wasn't really aware of what was going on about her. 'What did he want?'

'Just to discuss something that happened in Cumberland,' Judy replied.

'Nothing serious, I hope?'

'For goodness sake, Mother, if it had been, wouldn't I have told you about it?'

Prudence looked doubtfully at her daughter. Then she turned to Nick. 'I do think you ought to telephone your parents and tell them you're back from Spain and fit and well.'

'Yes, I must,' agreed Nick unenthusiastically, remembering that – under Judy's guidance – he'd never actually told them that he was going . . .

Judy said: 'I've decided to return with Nick and spend a day or two with Aunt Thelma and Uncle Patrick.'

'I'm sure they'd love to have you.' Prudence frowned. 'But didn't you tell me you were going up to Oxford to stay with Ingrid?'

'I said I might.'

'I could have sworn you were quite positive. Sometimes I think my memory's getting worse.'

'Impossible.'

'Whatever will Nick think, if you talk like that? . . . You know, I was in a hurry to do something, but for the life of me I can't remember what.'

'Go to Harrods and buy some steak for lunch.'

'That's what it was!'

After Prudence had left, Nick said: 'I'm glad you're coming back home with me.'

'I didn't have much option, did I? Left on your own, you'd blurt out everything that's happened and cause endless unnecessary problems.'

'But you'll have no difficulty at all in pulling the wool right over the parents' eyes?'

'Of course not.'

He laughed.